BLACKWATER MORNINGS

THE BARDO TRILOGY - 3

MALA NAIDOO

Naidoo, Mala

Title: *Blackwater Mornings*

ISBN :

978-0-6488090—4-3 (Print)

978-0-6488090-3-6 (eBook)

ABOUT THE AUTHOR

Mala Naidoo is an Australian author. She was born in South Africa during the apartheid era which is the impetus for her fictional stories that take on a life of their own when the creative muse beckons. Mala's novels and short-stories empower the voiceless by recalling forgotten voices that speak through the values and culture, angst and joy, of her characters' life situations and choices. This creates connections to a moment in time, an event or conversation, highlighting the universality of our existence.

For teachers — making a difference everyday

Conceal me what I am, and be my aid
For such disguise as haply shall become
The form of my intent.
~ Twelfth Night – William Shakespeare

Blackwater Ridge Performing Arts Academy was home to Viola, yet this time trepidation sullied the joy of her return.

Rob Dwyer called her to take on the acting principal seat during his time away. He trusted her, but she did not trust his decision. Viola's frequent departures from her home-based school at Blackwater Ridge would not make her the preferred candidate by some. Each time she had a vigilante mission, she left with Rob's blessing and the hope that she would return. Viola was his best music teacher and role model who drew parents and students into her positive, giving aura. He knew nothing of her vigilante justice activities. A white lie, and Rob's trust kept her secret intact.

Both her roles as a passionate music teacher and vigilante justice seeker had to coexist to be true to her values and beliefs. Rob was her Australian father figure. His exemplary leadership helped hone her skills as a leader in any role she held.

Rob's surgery, scheduled two days before Blackwater Ridge Performing Arts opened for the new academic year, meant she had to assume the position with immediate effect. His plan was to welcome her, introduce her in her new role to existing staff, but the body has a will of its own.

As leader, Rob's well-structured, pre-planned year received abundant gratitude from his hardworking staff. Health matters were beyond human timetabling, subject to the decree of health professionals.

Viola strolled down Illyria Square the morning after she arrived in Blackwater Ridge. She contemplated how she would address staff in the capacity of acting principal when she was away for three to six months in any academic year, more particularly in the last three years. As a part-time employee, she expected opposition on this ad hoc assumption of the position. Her relationship with long-standing staff was collegial in her years spent at Blackwater Ridge Performing Arts Academy. This position came with a range of unsettling possibilities, added to her fear that she would meet resistance from the few who tested Rob's leadership. She reminded herself that it was all of six weeks in the hot seat, and it was something she had to do for Rob more than anybody else.

The main street was quiet this early on a Sunday morning with the town coming to life around 10 am. She turned left into Cesario Lane and headed north in the Academy's direction.

Three cars gleamed in the car park in the pink flush of early morning light. She did not expect to see anyone on the campus today, least of all this early on a Sunday morning on the last day of the summer school break. Dedicated staff contributed to the Academy's reputation for delivering the finest education in the country.

Although she lived just two streets away from Illyria Square, she would need her car as she envisaged late nights and early mornings at the campus while Rob was out of action. It was time to reconnect with her psychologist, Olivia Sparks, to help her reclaim her courage to drive again. Her car stood covered in cobwebs in her underground parking bay at her apartment block.

She cautioned herself that she had to tackle one thing at a time. First, it was getting her head around the assistant principal position. Her reclusive nature was far from ideal with staff who wanted to be heard in their commitment to the Academy. Rob's advice lingered: *Deal with things as they arise. That is the only way to survive.*

Rob's tidy office made it easy to find what she required. A folder labelled *for attention Viola Bardo* stood up against the desktop computer. Inside she found a detailed plan laid out on how to run her first staff meeting, when to meet new staff, and from whom to order morning tea. Details filled page after page with careful attention on all she might need.

She walked out the office to inspect the gardens and buildings before she lost herself in studying the dense paperwork Rob had painstakingly prepared for her transition into his seat. The gardens around the administration block emitted a flurry of radiant colors from the roses Rob planted and maintained. They lined the main entrance to the building from the street in rainbow bouquets, filling the air with its floral scent. Viola paused and inhaled the surrounding freshness when she heard someone call out to her.

'Viola, lovely to see you!'

She looked up with hazy eyes to see a short figure approaching her. Her heart sang when she realized who it was.

'Fabian! How are you? Wow, it has been a while.'

He rushed to shake her hand.

'Not sure if I can hug my friend now that she is my principal.'

'Acting, that is all. A hug is good, and congratulations are in order. You are a new dad! You went off on paternity leave before I left.'

Fabian relished having his friend back and thanked her for remembering he was now a dad.

'This father-business is beautiful, but oh boy, tough! Sleepless nights are draining so expect to see me bleary-eyed some mornings. Let's go over to the staffroom, Andy's there with his latest recruit, a first year out on the field!'

'On a Sunday, That eager!'

'She comes highly recommended by the board so we might be the lucky ones.'

'Let's check her out! Coffee together might give us some insight.'

Fabian enjoyed the unchanged Viola and his instinct told him she would shine as acting head.

Andy turned to the door when he heard Viola's voice. He jumped up and rushed over to her. As Blackwater Ridge tradition had it, he enveloped her in a bear hug. Andy was the tallest teacher on staff. He stooped through doorways. His menacing appearance concealed a gentle heart.

'Viola! Welcome back! It is *so* good to see you! Charlotte Ainsworth is a new staff member in my department. Charlotte, this is our acting principal, Viola Bardo.'

Her first formally announced title hit the airwaves with a strange ring.

After the introductory civilities, Andy said he had an hour to finish his orientation with Charlotte. Fabian retorted that with teaching each day was a reorientation to a new set of happenings.

'Take Fabian's words with a pinch of salt. We are fortunate to be teaching at Blackwater Ridge Performing Arts Academy, and with Viola back, the year will kick off to a splendid start. This Academy is heaven to a first-year teacher!'

Viola smiled without committing to all Andy said.

She returned to Rob's office to pore through his meticulous folder when a sealed envelope labelled *Confidential,* fell out.

Inside was a list of things she should be cautious of. One name caught her eye: Lawrence Hargreaves — board chairperson at the Academy.

Lawrence was a formidable personality in his early days on

the board. He wanted the Academy run to his set of standards. Age mellowed him but he had an unpredictable nature. Viola never mingled with the board as a part-time teacher. All she knew of the board's members came through the grapevine. Now she would have to engage with Lawrence Hargreaves.

Rob cautioned her without mentioning a name that one individual was unhappy with his choice of acting head. He included that overwhelming joy was expressed by staff that she would head the Academy during his absence. One resistant individual was one too many in her book. She did not need names, the less she knew would not disturb her sleep.

Rob prioritized an impending marriage between his gardening maintenance and canteen staff. He encouraged her to attend the nuptials with staff and students. Two home visits, one to support a student whose father was away serving the armed forces, and another whose home was ravaged by recent bush fires needed her urgent attention. The family were currently living in makeshift accommodation while their home was being rebuilt.

Dear, compassionate Rob had all bases covered, including watching her back.

The role of principal was far from the romantic notion she entertained as a child. Rob went more than the extra mile, but his sensitive nature left him vulnerable and sometimes misunderstood.

Under his copious advice on leadership matters, sat his words of encouragement:

Best wishes, you will do a sterling job!

- Rob

Viola snuck in a look at her music room. She missed the hours she spent there over the years. The piano beckoned. She kicked off her shoes, pulled her legs up onto the stool and played every sweet melody as they entered her head. Peace returned to her corner room, tucked away at the furthest end of the oval. Six weeks away from her students would be difficult. She had to schedule a separate meeting with her replacement music teacher.

Fabian dropped by to say he would see her tomorrow, and Andy asked her to join him at *Duke's Bar and Grill* for lunch.

It was a hot Sunday, typical of an Australian summer. The dry heat much like her childhood summers in Mozambique.

Over lunch, she told Andy about her exchange position in Athens and her short stint at the English college in Porto. He offered to drive her home, but she opted to walk back to her apartment.

'Thank you for your company, Andy. It feels like home with you and Fabian around. Do you have any advice for me for tomorrow's meeting?'

Andy was never one to gossip or stir up situations.

'Be yourself in all you do is the best advice I have. The rest you figure out as you go.'

'Rob said the same thing, thank you Andy.'

Viola walked home, mulling over why Andy had not taken on the acting principal role. He had far more experience than she did. Soon she would talk to him on that.

HER FIRST UNOFFICIAL day at Blackwater Ridge Performing Arts settled her anxiety in the welcome Fabian and Andy extended. Poetry brewed now that she was in a calmer zone.

> *beach summer days*
> *friendship and surf*
> *balmy nights beckon*
> *weekend joy*
> *now the morrow awaits...*

2

Blackwater Ridge, contrary to its name, was a genial
town.

It was a place Viola enjoyed returning to for brief
periods in the last three years. Academics and artists enjoyed the
peaceful surroundings of this coastal hamlet. The town's settled
population comprised ageing, old money residents who assumed
power and control of the town's unique identity.

Mayor Corey, in his late seventies, showed no inclination to
relinquish his position. Nobody showed interest in the role, and
longstanding residents accepted he would remain in the role until
he passed.

Blackwater Ridge gained notoriety for its prestigious small
university, one high performing public school, and the interna-
tionally acclaimed Blackwater Ridge Performing Arts Academy.
The Academy accepted and invited students of all faiths and
denominations with open arms. This made Blackwater Ridge a
desired residential location. Viola considered herself blessed to
have settled here, although she was away as often as she was
there in the last few years.

Duke's Bar and Grill, the social hub in town, attracted visitors from the city for a weekend getaway to savor Duke's prime rib-eye steak and cocktails. Orsino's Jazz Trio played every night of the week from seven to ten pm, and all afternoon until eleven pm on Saturdays.

Blackwater Ridge's quaint charm and serene surroundings attracted poets and novelists who chose to live on the town's outskirts. The graveyard on the north side of Illyria Square overlooked the sea, a pristine parkland resting place that some folk joked was the reason they would never leave the town.

One supermarket, one pharmacy, one butcher, one baker, and one small general hospital was all the town needed. Prime retail outlets passed down the generations of fathers and sons, and some daughters. Local cottage industries served the community on specialist needs from tailoring to catering.

Everybody knew everybody at Blackwater Ridge. Newcomers were welcome, but privacy, secrecy, or seclusion presided over the town all the way to its outskirts.

Boxing Day was the highlight of the year at Blackwater Ridge, a carnival day. Every resident had to attend, the only excuse for non-attendance was illness. It was a great day outdoors, a massive family picnic under the cerulean sky of this pristine beach town where the wind carried whispers of unspoken past secrets. If the day threatened rain, the local community hall was the Plan B option, where residents gathered for a day of laughter, song, dance, and games.

The town's name reflected its past as a coal mining town in the 1800s. The abandoned mine now fenced off, as town planners worked on refurbishing it as a museum. Its history was its people spanning many generations. People with a strong, loyal, community spirit determined to preserve the memory of their ancestry. Five years passed with not much movement on its completion. The river at the back of the abandoned mine, a winding body of black water, had been listed as condemned for its poisonous pollutants by Mayor Corey. Trespassers faced a hefty fine and community service.

The Adriatic Freeway was the only point of entry and exit to Blackwater Ridge. The town hall clock, a replica of Big Ben, chimed every hour from the days when the mine was operational. Mayor Corey adjusted the hourly chime to twice a day when a petition from the university board appealed to have it stopped. Locals and creatives living in the town center joined the movement for change. The mayor was dead against it, until forced to accept that the prestigious academic reputation of Blackwater Ridge was at risk because the gong disrupted examination weeks. For as long as the town existed, the gong signaled a suspension of activities. This pause, according to the narrative passed down, kept miners alert during their shift. The initial thunderous volume of the gong sounded like an hourly war siren in the town center. The younger generation did not adhere to halting activities at midday. Essential services proceeded in life threatening situations. Limiting the frequency of the gong was the only change Mayor Corey ever entertained.

SMALL, elite, sedate – Blackwater Ridge held an air of friendliness and dark secrets.

* * *

SUNRISE on the white sands of the seashore, the bluest sparkling water and gentle breeze or stillness, soothed tired, lonely, and aching souls. Viola sought many hours of restoration on Blackwater Ridge's beach. It calmed her, gave her clarity and purpose after her motor accident. Ten years had passed since her car accident left a woman wheelchair bound. Viola escaped to Blackwater Ridge when the city trapped her in a dark mental space, consumed by guilt. Her departure was not to reinvent herself, but to find a way to forgive herself. This way she would have the capacity to bring value to the lives of others. Viola kept in constant touch with the young woman who scaled a fence onto the freeway on a Friday night when her car struck the fleeing victim. The woman's unthinking act was her only means of escape from a violent partner pursuing her with a knife. After four years of daily visits to the woman, Viola moved to Blackwater Ridge with the young woman's blessing that she heal herself by moving away.

Tempest coerced Viola to join the ranks of vigilante investigator. How the mysterious Tempest found her online continued to baffle her. With music in her soul and justice pumping her blood, Viola fed her aching need to heal from the horrific memory of the accident.

This morning she had to face a full staff meeting as acting principal. The sea called out to her from her apartment balcony, and the early morning roar of waves brought confidence and clarity. A cool breeze billowed through her tangled hair, electrifying her spirit for whatever the day held.

She was the first one to arrive at the Academy; the carpark was disquietingly empty. It was an hour before her meeting. Fifteen minutes after her arrival, she received a text message from her father.

ABUNDANT BEST WISHES ARTISTA! You will be great.
   Much love as ever
   Papa XXX.
   She replied with two red hearts and three words, *call you later.*

ANDY'S WORDS RETURNED. *She had to be herself.* Without a doubt, authentic Viola Bardo was the only way she knew how to survive. Theatrical behavior annoyed her when she saw it in others. As much as the leadership role placed her on the academic stage at Blackwater Ridge Performing Arts Academy, she would remain true to her calling.

Yesterday on her way home after lunch with Andy, she stopped at the Cesario Lane Bakery and ordered blueberry muffins from Milsom Jones, for her first staff morning tea.

'I will have your order delivered and set up in the staffroom. This is a heavy load for you to carry down to the Academy. So glad you are here helping Rob out. Poor guy, hope he's going to get well soon.'

'Thank you Milsom. It's good to be back but I am holding onto Rob being brand new again soon.'

'That's the way! See you in the morning!'

As promised, Milsom delivered piping hot blueberry muffins and set them up in the staffroom, together with a beautiful bouquet of roses to welcome her back. This was the Blackwater Ridge that Viola called home. Folk in this town looked out for each other, celebrating victories, helping in times of financial crisis, and during emotional, vulnerable moments — a community everybody wanted and needed.

Andy popped his head in at the staffroom door.

'Wow! Are we having a party or what? It smells divine in here. Ready for your meeting Ms Bardo?'

He knew her as well as Rob did. She was not one for pomp and show. Today would be a difficult one, but he knew she would sail through.

'You should be in the seat Andy, not me. Why aren't you?'

'Long story there. I will tell you over coffee someday. Break a leg. You will be fine! See you in the meeting.'

She watched him leave, uneasy with why he showed no interest in the position as a man with vast experience. Blackwater Ridge for all its wonderful ways had some secrets that needed to be dragged out from behind its rock.

Staff trickled in from around 9:15 am. Some rushed to Viola for a hug and others told her how relaxed she looked, and that time away seemed to be essential for an energized start to the year. New staff nodded nervously. None of them were familiar, as they had joined the Academy after she had left for Athens.

Almost every staff member brought in a plate of home-baked treats for tea. It was more a family gathering than the start of an academic year staff meeting.

Her meeting was a cheerful, resounding success, with everyone happy to see her. With part one behind her, Viola felt she could handle whatever came her way.

Rob faced opposition from a few staff members whenever he instituted new policies handed down by the board. Those who opposed him felt he was too lenient in not contesting the board's requirements on new policies. Rob never debated with any of his staff, but had the tendency to retreat to his office, seeking solace in solitude. Viola knew this to be detrimental to his leadership and cautioned herself to avoid doing the same. She preferred to tackle things and diffuse them as they arose. Her leadership would be as she led students in her classroom. It served her well.

Delegation earned her kudos when she asked for volunteers to run school assemblies and one staff member to be present at all her meetings with the board. She valued transparency over secrecy, but her vigilante role operated under a different set of values. It would remain her tightly guarded secret.

Viola returned to her apartment that afternoon lighter than she imagined possible. All she had to do now was ask for an assistant in her capacity as acting principal.

3

Rob's surgery was over, the nail-biting wait ended, but he asked his wife to pass on to the staff at the Academy that he was not accepting visitors for another week. He included Viola in the exclusion period, sending alarm bells off that something was amiss, not quite as Ingrid conveyed.

No calls, no visits.

Viola scheduled a meet-up with Ingrid at Dukes. Dukes was quiet that afternoon. The heat sent everyone down to the beach for a splash.

'Thank you for meeting me, Viola.'

'Thank you, Ingrid, for agreeing to see me during this stressful time for you. I understand Rob needs time to himself after major surgery.'

Ingrid sighed and nodded, avoiding eye contact with Viola.

'Sometimes, Rob is headstrong about things he cannot control, and he would rather not have staff seeing him in pain. He is on morphine and dips in and out of wakefulness. His specialist has advised that he should be off his feet for at least six weeks.'

Ingrid's face was more lined than Viola recalled. They last met a year ago at a staff dinner.

'As much as I want him back at Blackwater Ridge Academy, I respect he must adhere to his medical team's advice. If there is anything I can do to help you during this time, please ask.'

'That's truly kind of you, Viola. I have a full plate now but must go it alone as Rob expects. It is a blessing though that he does not have to stress about the work front, thanks to you.'

Ingrid was more tight-lipped this afternoon than Viola expected, but it pleased her that Rob had peace of mind with her running the Academy. The truth on his post-operative recovery left Viola doubtful. Rob could be overprotective with the women in his life, seeing himself as the knight in shining armor, always there to save everyone but himself.

Ingrid left for the hospital, and Viola walked to the front desk to speak to Duke's owner, Ellis McCrae.

'It's great to have you drop by so often. How's Ingrid doing? Those two are inseparable, it must be such a strained time for her having Rob in hospital for this length of time.'

Ellis McCrae's concern echoed the love and care of the townsfolk at Blackwater Ridge. Everybody stepped up when someone was in need. This made the town a warm home for Viola. It's the people that make a place home, and her joy here was greater than her angst.

'She seems to cope, or so she says, but is rather wan. Stress takes its toll. I will be happy when Rob's out of pain and on his feet again. Has much changed since I've been away this past quarter? I notice little except Rob's absence from the Academy.'

'The usual, nothing overly concerning, although I do have this niggling nervousness with the caravans coming in next week. We love the boost they bring to our trade when they pass through, but a sense of unease pervades whenever this parade arrives. Do you remember Marty's daughter? Well, the word is that she took off with one caravanner without telling her father, poor Marty!'

'Oh dear, I did not know that, yes I have met Marty. And still no word from her, right? Is Marty sure she joined the caravan community?'

'Who knows around here? I've heard nothing different lately.'

Viola pondered why this happened and that there was no follow-up.

'Get the mayor involved to drum support from the police department in Sydney to come over. It limits us with one police commissioner running the operation.'

Ellis was a sixth-generation resident at Blackwater Ridge. He lived through the highs and lows of the town. Old residents prided themselves on their crime free town.

'Marty is a bit of a private guy if you remember. Heavy police presence in the town is not in the spirit of Blackwater Ridge. We try to avoid that side of things as you know. Besides, Marty's girl was in her mid-twenties. We must do our bit and bite our tongues while the caravans pass through, they have rights, and we have no proof of them being involved in Marty's girl's departure.'

Viola wandered whether Marty's daughter was complicit or not in leaving Blackwater Ridge without a word to anyone. Because she was not a minor, her whereabouts went unchecked.

'I could ask the staff at Blackwater Ridge Academy to keep their eyes and ears open during this period when the caravans roll through town.'

'Good idea! The young ones are restless, and newcomers excite them where they lose a sense of reason and propriety, forgetting the expert advice given by well-meaning parents.'

Viola laughed, 'I've been there, Ellis, so I appreciate what you're saying.'

Ellis refused to accept that the lovely Ms Bardo could do wrong.

'You would've been a saint, in your day! You have so much love for your father. That tells me you would never have done what Marty's daughter did.'

'It's a good thing the caravans are only here for a week when they pass through. Let's hope this year things will be calm, and they don't tempt our young ones into silliness.'

'It tested Marty losing his wife when the girl was only six years old. He raised Alison with no help, struggling along the way, but he did the best he could. Poor guy! That's the gratitude he gets!'

'Let's hope she returns, sometime soon, or perhaps we could ask the crowd coming in next week, if they have seen her.'

'Easier said than done, Viola. But we must not give up.'

* * *

VIOLA'S CURIOSITY sent her on a mental investigative hunt to know more about the caravanner's who pulled into town on their sojourn.

Ellis said the colorful parade on the main road, to the left of Dukes, was a spectacle each year when they arrived. Viola had never seen this sight before, being out of town on one of Tempest's missions in the past three years. According to Ellis, the caravans passed through around mid-February. This would be their third trip passing through town. The parade of twelve cara-vans split into two groups of six, one parked off at the trailer park, and the other six at the beachfront. Both locations were within walking distance from the town center. Ellis recommended avoiding the beach during the week of their stay. The caravanning families were large and took over most of the space and amenities at the beach. It was a town on wheels. Home schooling happened on board with parents liaising with the education department to ensure they followed the requirements for the states and territories where their children would sit for their final examinations. Their laid-back lifestyle, and love of the earth suggested there was nothing to fear with their arrival. Peaceful folk on their perpetual journey across the country. Viola's interest peaked; she would keep a close eye on the visitors when they arrived.

PLACIDO CALLED to check in on his Artista.

'Meu filho, it's still not a home around here without you! How are things at Blackwater Ridge? Boring, I hope!' Placido chuckled.

'You will be happy to know, papa, that things are running far more smoothly than I expected. Everybody is so helpful to ensure things run as Rob would have wanted, so far from boring!'

'What can I say, it's your warm personality that brings out the best in people. I am happy to hear you are settling in well!'

He told her Matthew and Jungen were coming over to spend Easter with him.

'Ariel is good company, but a bit too private like Helena. I need the energy that Matthew and Jungen carry.'

'Enjoy the quiet, papa, as much as you can.'

'Has Helena called you since you got back to Blackwater Ridge?'

'I actually owe mother a call. She does not know I'm not with you now.'

'You must let her know. Give her my regards when you speak. I have a tiny bit of news to share.'

'That sounds intriguing. What is it?'

'I am invited to join a reflection hour on *The Artist's Channel* next week.'

'That's wonderful news, papa! You have many more strokes left in your brush.'

'Oh, you flatter me! This old man needs to retire soon.'

'You are a valued artist. Don't shy away from that!'

Every achievement her father gained made her proud that he persisted in the face of personal challenges. They parted, with Viola complaining about a desk load of paperwork she had to wade through that morning.

An hour and a half later Viola stared out at the star-laden night sky from her open balcony door. Welcome solitude, after her wild days in Porto. Placido was happy, and that meant every-thing to her. Rob was going to be ok, she convinced herself, and staff towed the line on all her decisions.

Viola counted her blessings and scribbled a gratitude Elfchen in her journal.

starry
bright night
home at last
soothed by sea sounds.
happy!

4

———————

The first week at Blackwater Ridge was hectic but on a positive note everything ran to schedule. Rob's time-lines were accurate and his predictions on the mark. Viola sailed through her daily academic events.

Five weeks to go and she would be at the piano keyboard again, singing along with her students. She ached for time with them. The days were tight, and it exhausted her by day's end to attempt sneaking in a few bars before she headed home.

Her office door invited a steady stream of staff and parents, most on an appointment basis. This left her with a mountain of take-home work. She learned early in her teaching career that an educator's day never ends. Many after hours work and constant learning made teachers eternal scholars. It was a lifestyle that had to be embraced with passion. Reflecting on the days' happenings was just as important as planning. Her day ran like clockwork, but exhaustion eroded sleep. She thrived on the adrenaline that surged in being of service. But she was glad this was a short-lived leadership thrust upon her.

* * *

Charlotte Ainsworth arrived at Viola's door without an appointment and somehow got past her secretary without a fuss. Charlotte's flushed face and red nose meant trouble. Viola hurried her into the office and shut the door behind her. The floodgates opened as Charlotte uttered her apology for barging in.

'I did not know what else to do. May I take just five minutes of your time, Ms Bardo?'

From the pained sob and unstoppable flood of tears, Viola knew this would take more than five minutes. She could not turn away a newly appointed novice teacher. Rob would do the same.

'Is this a school matter, Ms Ainsworth?'

Formality was paramount to avoid losing control of the situation. Rob teased her about her rigid adherence to formality. Her mother said it saved anyone thinking they had an advantage in troublesome situations.

Viola's stern look was enough to start another river of tears from the young woman who appeared barely older than the current year twelve cohort.

'I did not mean to upset you with that question. I adhere to protocol and report as things are without speculation or erroneous interpretation. Personal matters have to be passed on to the Academy's counselor and union representative, depending on the nature of the issue.'

'It's not you that has upset me. It's Fabian.'

'Fabian?'

'Yes, we were both on yard duty on the soccer field, during lunch yesterday and he was rather brusque in telling me I needed to develop my behavior management strategy. This was within earshot of year twelve students.'

'That seems out of character with the Fabian I know. Have you approached him on this? What triggered this reaction from him?'

Viola had no patience for emotional outbursts without context.

She noticed Charlotte Ainsworth's trembling hands.

'I can't talk to him... I don't know what made him so angry. I don't know how I can continue working with him, to be honest.'

'I am sorry to hear this. You should see Ruth Beasley, our counselor, to help you with the anxiety you are displaying. This appears to be a personal matter, but I will speak to Fabian to gauge if I can salvage your professional relationship. Remember, we are never *friends* with *everyone* in this profession or any other for that matter. We are different because we are human.'

Rob's private brief on staff issues warned her to be forthright and fair. Personal matters had to be delegated to the counselor for arbitration if needed. Only when all options failed was the union to be reeled in, and that was up to the warring teachers, not her nor the board.

Viola watched Charlotte Ainsworth leave the room. Something had to have irked Fabian if he reacted as she said. As much as Fabian was a colleague with whom she had the odd social drink, if he was wrong, he had to be called in on it. Her secretary sent a message to Fabian to see her.

Fabian's stony face peered in through her office door, twenty minutes after Charlotte left. Viola had never seen a cloud over this man before.

'Come in Mr Bennett. Please shut the door and take a seat.'

This was awkward for Viola for a few seconds.

'Look, I don't beat around the bush. Please drop the formality, what's with, 'Mr Bennett,' it's just us in here. That young Charlotte is a whiner.'

'I will treat this with the respect and formality I give Rob Dwyer. Please understand this.'

'As you say.'

'Charlotte Ainsworth is your colleague, a member of staff,

not a student. I urge you to refrain from your use of derogatory statements, please. Tell me what transpired between you.'

'What did she say to you?'

'You know I can't reveal this until I hear what you have to say on the issue.'

'Really? I feel like I'm the accused kindergarten kid.'

'Far from it. If you want a union rep present, do so.'

'Geez, are you kidding?'

'Let me hear your truth, please.'

Viola knew Fabian was not a troublemaker. He would want this squashed. It wounded him that his mate Viola pulled rank over him. She would not bend to him. Truth and justice were a priority.

'You know, junior teachers – always on their cell phones! They rarely give full attention on duty.'

Viola raised her hand.

'Tell me, what happened without judgement. Just the bald details, please. If this is not possible, I will ask for a written statement from both of you.'

'That won't be necessary. Justice and a fair go, I get it!'

Fabian took a deep breath. This was a man she did not know, angry and condemning.

'I was on duty with Charlotte, on the soccer field during the lunch break yesterday. I advised her we both had to be vigilant as the lads could get rough and injure each other.'

Viola nodded with her hands clasped on her lap under the desk.

'Charlotte's cell phone rang, and she walked off the field to take the call in private. In the forty-five-minute break, she turned away from her duty post for twenty minutes. I let it go for the first ten minutes and then approached her. Well, what do you know, she was on a video call on her very large-screened phone with a shirtless bloke prancing on the other end!'

Fabian's eyeballs bulged out his skull. Viola poured him a glass of water.

She understood Fabian's irritation. He held similar values to her on duty of care, as expected of an upstanding teacher. But going close enough to peer at Charlotte's phone screen was another issue.

'This will not resolve today. I have to have you both in here to settle this if that's what you want to do.'

'I might as well tell you I did butt in to tell her she had to end her call to pick up her duty. Please don't tell me I should not have done that!'

Fabian folded his arms and stared across the table, waiting for Viola's response.

'Thank you for the details. You had a right to tell Charlotte Ainsworth to return to her duty. We have to resolve this tomorrow.'

'May I leave?'

Viola heard Fabian's resigned tone. He knew as well as her that there were errors on both sides of the argument. He left without another word.

Her first staff clash happened early in her temporary leadership tenure. Rob was in recovery and out of reach as her sounding board. Andy and Fabian were close, talking to Andy was out of the question. Viola mulled over calling the union for advice and tossed it aside. She had to make peace between her two staff members with a lesson for both.

A FRAZZLED VIOLA walked home at 5:30 pm. This ended up being her most tough day on the job. People matters needed a delicate yet firm hand. Finding that balance sucked the energy from her. She wished Lorenza were just a telephone call away, but she had to deal with this on her own.

Her glass of gin sat on the kitchen counter. A beach walk was the balm for her troubled thoughts. The beachfront, deserted on a summer evening, was odd. She looked at the time; it was 8 pm and most folks were home having dinner. A young couple romanced behind the sand dunes. She walked further down the beach and plonked herself on the warm sand. A few deep inhalations cleared her head, and she imagined a conversation with the wise Rob Dwyer.

Both need a reprimand. Fabian will have to accept that his approach lacked careful thought. They should apologize and get over this impasse. A schoolyard mentality is for students. Think of the lesson you want them to have, Ms Bardo. Keep up the formality here.

In her imagined conversation with Rob, she had not expected to hear him speak of maintaining formality.

5

The caravans arrived at Blackwater Ridge overnight. All twelve caravans formed a laager at the beach. This time, none headed to the caravan park.

Dukes opened earlier when the caravans came to town. Viola stopped for a takeaway coffee and noticed that Orsino's Jazz Band played every night, including Sundays in the week the caravan party was around. They played for an extra hour each weekday night, to entice the visitors to come into the town center to bolster Backwater Ridge's economy. Ellis ensured he took care of the visitors.

The caravan population brought color, music, culture, and dance to the usually quiet hamlet tucked along the coast, surrounded by mountains, hidden in secrets.

Ellis called out to Viola when she walked through the door. He had a group of men around him she had never seen before.

'Come over, come and meet our visitors.'

Viola glanced at her watch to check if she could fit in a quick conversation before her morning school assembly. She left home a little later than usual this morning.

'A quick chat is all I can manage, sorry. I have a school assembly on first thing this morning.'

'Aww, come on, you are the head, so you can be late. Gentlemen, this is Blackwater Ridge's Performing Arts Academy's acting principal. I give you Ms Viola Bardo!'

Ellis drummed his fingers on the table, and Viola's cheeks turned deep red.

The older man among them smiled.

'Ah *Ms* Bardo, how can a pretty thing like you manage that?'

'Careful, Luis, this is a woman with power. She will have you booked for detention if you talk down to her.' Another graybeard laughed.

'Enough gentleman, Viola is doing a sterling job filling in for Rob Dwyer.'

'Just joking around, ma'am, don't mean to be rude.'

Viola smelt the stale, lingering odor of whiskey on his breath.

'You are way too generous with your introduction, Ellis. I'm a rookie in this position, so hold the praise.'

'Modest too, just the way I like me ladies,' Luis winked.

'Enough of that now, how about you show some respect?'

Viola took no offence, if Ellis sat around chatting with the men, she knew they were not a nasty lot. She laughed it off and walked over to collect her standing order of coffee from the young barista.

'Well gentlemen, I hope you have a wonderful stay while you are at Blackwater Ridge, and Ellis will feed you well, that's for sure.'

All four men stood up and wished Viola a pleasant day at work.

She smiled, happy that manners did indeed *maketh the man*. Ellis had a positive impact on this rough on the road community.

One man, the older tease, said his name was Luis Tennant.

'I'm sure I'll see you all again. Take care, now.'

As Viola walked away, she heard Luis Tennant whisper,

'What a lady. She must be a fine teacher, too. We could do with someone of her caliber in our traveling community.'

* * *

ANDY RAN the morning assembly with fine attention to detail and some lively music from the school orchestra to wake up the sleepy heads in the audience.

Charlotte Ainsworth sidled up to Viola at the end of the assembly.

'Good morning, Ms Bardo, any chance we might resolve the matter today?'

'Once I get back to my office, I will have a look when I can slot you both in for a meeting.'

'Fabian and I are free after recess if that fits in with your day.'

Viola thanked Charlotte, sensing her urgency to resolve the matter. That was a good sign for any administrator.

A quick glance at the timetable for the day confirmed Charlotte's and Fabian's availability. Her secretary informed them about the post recess meeting. An hour before her meeting, a stressed Ingrid Dwyer called Viola. Rob had a heart attack in the early hours of the morning and was in high care. No visitors allowed. Viola felt a ton of bricks collapse on her. She suppressed her gasp. Ingrid did not need to hear her anxiety about not being able to stay on for longer than scheduled. She had to calm Ingrid.

'Think of it this way, while it is a difficult time, at least it happened while he was in the hospital, and not at home. Rob is in safe hands and you must trust that.'

'I know, and Rob's lucky to have you holding the fort together for him.'

This unexpected news threw Viola. She had plans, many plans.

'Please keep him in your prayers and ask the staff to do the same.'

'We will. May I come over to see you this evening?'

Ingrid's lengthy pause confirmed that today was not a good time.

'How about you let me know when you would like me to come over.'

'Thank you for understanding, I will be in touch.'

An email to staff on Rob's current health status was all she could fit in today. Word got around fast and some would already be privy to this information. It was her task to subvert detrimental speculations on whether Rob would return to the Academy. After several redrafts of her email, she hit send.

* * *

THE MEETING with Charlotte and Fabian was in ten minutes.

Charlotte arrived first and Fabian followed two minutes later.

'Thank you both for agreeing to meet this way. First, do either of you want a union representative or a neutral third-party present.'

'No, not me,' Fabian chipped in, and Charlotte agreed she did not want a union rep sitting in, but asked who the neutral third-party would be.

'HR or the school secretary.'

Both wanted no outside intervention, and happily accepted that Viola would chair the meeting.

Viola sat back in Rob's chair, crossed her palms, and looked at Charlotte Ainsworth.

'Ms Ainsworth, it is my duty as acting principal here at Blackwater Ridge Performing Arts Academy to ensure your debut year as a full-time teacher is a smooth and enjoyable one for you.'

'Thank you, Ms Bardo,' Charlotte whispered with a furtive glance in Fabian's direction.

'However, when professionalism crosses the line, I have to intervene with due attention to all sides. There is no other way to say it, except that duty of care when allocated yard duty requires just that – undivided attentiveness, unless negotiated with the partner teacher on duty. This would be only if an emergency arose, not for personal activities.' She dared not use the word *frivolous* as Fabian implied.

Charlotte turned scarlet. Her head dropped to her chest.

'Fabian Bennett, you are a respected staff member and my colleague for many years. It is acceptable and within your jurisdiction as a senior teacher on duty that you correct a teacher. But the manner is as important as the message. Respectful communication is non-negotiable. This is where you fell short by talking down to Ms Ainsworth with students within earshot. If you believe my interpretation of the situation is incorrect, speak now, please.'

Viola studied their faces. Both were a picture of pity and awkwardness, quite embarrassed by this respectful dressing down. The hallway clock ticked louder than she had heard it before, admonishing the silence in the room.

Charlotte raised her hand.

'I was wrong to step away from yard duty to attend to a private call that was not urgent. For this I am sincerely sorry, and I hope Mr Bennett will accept my apology as my lesson learnt. I have no excuse.'

'Thank you for your honesty, Ms Ainsworth.'

Viola looked at Fabian from above her reading glasses.

'Mr Bennett, what is your response?'

He turned to face Charlotte.

'I apologize for my brusque handling of the situation, and swear with my hand on heart that I did not intend to be rude to you. I have no right to speak to you or any member of staff with anger.'

Fabian's crestfallen look tugged at Viola's heartstrings. Both people in front of her were good human beings, caught in a teacher's rushed day.

'Thank you, Fabian, for saying that, and thank you for being forthright with us, Viola.'

All formality, now gone with the wind as Viola's Gen Y teacher relaxed.

'Are you both sure you want this resolved this way, with an apology from both sides?'

Both nodded, eager to be over this.

'If you can resume an amicable working relationship, then my job is done.'

Fabian reached out to shake Charlotte's hand. She fell into sobbing, which Viola feared would happen. Fabian withdrew his hand in shocked surprise.

'I am so sorry to have hurt you this way. How can I make it up to you?'

'You have,' she said in a teary voice. 'My tears are my relief. I expected this to drag on.'

Fabian looked at Viola to help him understand.

'I am so glad you both chose a swift resolution to this matter. You should go back to your classrooms now. Have a good rest of the day.'

Viola, relieved that they did not drag this out, returned to a mountain of work waiting for her attention.

One problem solved, cleared the way for other urgent matters.

What waited in the wings was about to add another weight on her short-lived lightened shoulders.

6

iola walked down to Duke's half an hour earlier for a bacon and egg breakfast. She needed the protein fuel after pulling an all-nighter wading through urgent reports.

Ellis was on the telephone. His lowered tones, the usual pink glow drained from his plump cheeks, worried her.

He turned to Viola, eyes raised, running his fingers through his hair.

'Ellis, what's happened?'

He shook his head, coming to terms with what he just heard.

'It's Nadia, Milsom Jones granddaughter. She's missing. The family just discovered that she has not slept in her bed. Cesario Lane Bakery is closed this morning. Milsom has never shut the bakery before. He's beside himself with worry. His daughter had to be sedated by Dr. Joubert. This reminds me of Marty's girl's unexplained departure. When this gets out, the townsfolk will be edgy and lock themselves away.'

Viola listened to the anxiety in Ellis' voice. He knew the Jones family from childhood. Nadia's mother grew up around him. To mother and daughter, he was Uncle Ellis.

'How old is Nadia?'

'Sixteen. She was having some problems at school in Sydney, and her mother brought her over to Blackwater Ridge for a while. Nadia has been living with her father ever since her parents divorced but came to her mother and grandfather every school holiday.'

'When did the parents' divorce?'

'Eighteen months ago.'

'This situation is still a recent change for Nadia. Tricky age.'

Ellis looked at Viola, amazed at her old head. She had no children of her own, yet she understood how young people reacted to challenges. Teaching gave her a maternal edge.

'I wonder whether she chose to run away, or someone abducted her? Where would she go?'

'The family should speak to the bus station commander, and check with her father, if Nadia's mother hasn't done that yet.'

The telephone rang, and Ellis excused himself. His hunched shoulders told her it was not good news.

'That was Milsom. Their neighbor's share house boarder is also missing.'

'Oh dear, perhaps the girls ran away together. You must pass this on to the police commissioner.'

'Nobody must know, to avoid other young women running off. Youngsters will find some entertainment in this. I hope it is just a prank, and that they return soon.'

'Hang onto that thought Ellis, I have to rush.'

'Your breakfast?'

'I'll grab a coffee and stop on my way home this afternoon to check in with you on the girls. Call me if you need help with anything. I'm a mean coffee maker, can't cook to save my soul, but coffee, that's my thing!'

Ellis smiled in appreciation of Viola's kind humor. He needed it.

A hurried meeting alerted the Academy's teaching staff to the current situation, and all had to keep the situation under wraps for now. Ellis was happy for staff to be added to the watchful eyes around the town. On no account were students to be told. Nadia was aloof ever since her arrival in Blackwater Ridge, forming no close friendships at the public school she attended. No one was likely to talk.

Viola mulled over what Ellis said. The girl had a bout of depression. She noted this in her journal. Her investigative mind was an inbuilt mechanism. There was much to mend on the school front. Her journal was at the ever ready to record dates, times, and events, as she heard them.

* * *

THE ACADEMY'S part-time music teacher was on a sick day, and Viola jumped at the opportunity to cover a class or two for her. Her workload was at full capacity, but she needed the breath of the classroom.

Today was piano day for senior students. The dance in Viola's step was irrepressible when she greeted the adoring eyes before her.

'Ms Bardo! Are you back permanently to teach us now? Please say yes!'

A bright-eyed lass, an accelerant student in her advanced classical music class, smiled at Viola.

'No, dear Misty, I'm here as cover for Ms Jedda just today.'

'Please come back. Ms Jedda is so hard that I'm afraid to make a mistake while playing,' a tall lad complained.

'Now you know I won't entertain any complaints about your teacher. You are lucky to have her!'

An instant hush fell over in the room.

Soon music floated out onto the corridor, and Viola, lost in the hour, sailed through the keys, and notes in tune with her students. The depressing news she heard early that morning slipped out of conscious thought for a while.

Andy turned up at Viola's office unannounced around mid-afternoon and shut the door behind him.

'Sorry, Viola. I did not mean to barge in. You are busy all day that I had to grab you now.'

'What's wrong, Andy? I have never seen you so stressed before.'

'I don't know how much you're aware of what's happened. My wife called an hour ago to say that her niece is missing. It seems she might have left in the early hours of the morning, before the family rose for the day.'

'What? That's three young women! Did you tell your wife about Milsom's granddaughter and their neighbor?'

'Only after she told me her niece disappeared.'

Andy's guilt for letting out what Viola asked staff to keep private was obvious with his spurious, heavy breathing. Towns-folk were schooled on being tight-lipped.

'Ellis asked that staff keep this quiet until there were some leads, but your situation is an exception.'

'My wife knows not to say a word to anyone, not even to her brother.'

'Good, I will talk to Ellis later although I suspect he might know.'

'Blackwater Ridge is a small family community, after all. Some secrets are hard to contain.'

'I know. How old is your wife's niece?'

'She turned sixteen last week.'

'I see.'

WHEN ANDY LEFT, Viola pondered for a second what the connection might be that two of the three girls, aged sixteen, were from the public high school. The third girl was still a mystery.

* * *

A RESTLESS MIND SPURNS SLEEP.

Viola tossed, turned, and got out of bed to pick up her journal from the lounge room coffee table. She sketched the details across two pages on the hair coloring, height, and size of each girl. The two known girls were of similar stature, with dark brown hair. The girls were homebodies she gathered from Ellis.

People did not go missing in Blackwater Ridge. There was historically only one incident, prior to the speculation around Marty's daughter. That was during the town's mining heydays. Itinerant miners passed through taking on contract work and moved on. In the late 1800s a nineteen-year-old miner, Mitch Blank, disappeared, with no foul play reported. His bloated body washed up a month after his disappearance downstream on the banks of Blackwater River. It appeared he went over to the river after an argument with his manager. How he fell in went unexplained, and nobody questioned it.

This set Viola wondering if the girls had gone to the forbidden mine site or had someone slipped into three homes that night and took the girls? Milsom's Rottweiler would have raised hell if that was the case.

She erased the thought. It seemed impossible. Or did somebody slip into town without Ellis noticing? He was the eyes and ears of Blackwater Ridge. Townsfolk turned to him for advice rather than the priest or police commissioner. They trusted him. Viola had more questions to ask him. Her justice head was hard to quieten.

It was watch, listen, and wait. Somebody might let slip some crucial piece of information.

There was nothing she could do.

Poetry whispered through her disturbed thoughts.

> *three young women gone*
> *as townsfolk slept and dreamed*
> *free will or taken?*

A TROT down to the beach at almost two in the morning was not ideal under the current climate.

The white expanse of ocean, silvery under a shadowed moon, frothed and rolled out, stretching onto the shore.

The view of the ocean under the looming moon revealed that the caravans had left.

* * *

VIOLA CALLED HER FATHER. She needed to hear his warm caramel tones. He picked up her call in his office.

'Artista, this is a surprise! You usually send a text message to tell me you're calling. Something wrong, meu filho? It's late, why are you awake at this ungodly hour?'

Viola sighed, 'Too much on my mind, papa and I miss you.'

'How is your new position? All going as expected?'

'This acting principal role is hard. Some things are good, and some things stretch me like a contortionist.'

'Ah, life! You need some caramel popcorn. But these days you avoid sugar.'

'Yes, too much sugar makes one age too soon.'

'What hocus-pocus! Age indeed! Well, on a pleasant note I have more good news.'

'Please share, I need good news, you are on a roll these days!'

'In a strange collaboration of the stars, after the problems here over Christmas and the media hype, there's been a surge of interest in Galleria Bardo.'

'That's wonderful to hear. Tell me more.'

'Ariel and I are collaborating on a few pieces, and a young Saudi prince has shown interest in our work and has commissioned a generous supply of artwork to set up his latest marital palace. I can kiss bad debt goodbye, meu filho, spruce up the gallery and leave you a generous sum.'

'What do you mean? Leave me a generous sum! I'll have none of that talk from you!'

'Reality is something we cannot avoid. You know the old ticker is not the best these days.'

'Nonsense! All you need is a bit of exercise. Walking is good for you.'

'I will open the gallery three days a week to the public and that fee will upkeep the place.'

'My creative papa has finally grown a business head! Bravo! Ariel is the right influence for you, I think.'

'Ariel? No, she lives with her head in the clouds. But she is a lovely spirit around here that keeps me motivated.'

Viola, eager to tell Placido about the happenings in her world, held her tongue out of respect for Ellis and Milsom.

Their conversation abruptly ended when an overseas buyer called her father.

7

Dukes was the information hub in the town.

Ellis, the Godfather of Blackwater Ridge, the protector, the shield, and advisor to those who struggled with life's challenges.

Three young women disappeared that morning from Blackwater Ridge. Something had to be done to find them before the news hit the headlines and sent the town's folk into a self-elected lockdown.

Ellis was not in when Viola went over for her coffee and the latest news. She arrived hoping he would have a significant positive lead on where the young women might be.

A barista she had never seen before stood at the coffee machine.

'Good morning, is Ellis coming in this morning?'

The barista peered over the top of the counter. He was a short man who could pass for a school kid at a rapid glance.

'I'm sorry ma'am, he said he will be in at 9 am.'

'Is everything okay? My name is Viola Bardo, acting principal at Blackwater Ridge Performing Arts Academy,' she detested title dropping, and this was a mouthful, but she had to clarify who she was to get the barista to tell her more. 'I spoke to Ellis yesterday morning.'

The short man bent lower. His head barely visible behind the counter. Then his inaudible whisper forced Viola to lean toward him. A clandestine sight to any passerby!

'He's down at the station ma'am, checking up on matters, you know... on the… situation. He said only to tell you where he was and not to say a word to anyone else who came in this morning.'

Ellis and his regular barista were in a meeting with the police commissioner. A one-man operation took care of safety and justice issues in this small tight-knit community. The commissioner's doors were open to anybody who called. Law and order needed little attention, it seemed, which allowed him to organize community events, senior citizens' morning coffee, and every other event in town. The ladies were always eager to bake a batch of scones for a catch up on town gossip. Who got married, who was having a baby, who graduated? Now the conversations would turn to darker things such as runaways and crime.

Viola grabbed her coffee, thanked the barista, and hastened to the station.

All three men in earnest conversation, were unaware that she poked her head through the door. She waited outside for Ellis.

Relief washed over his troubled face when he saw her.

'Good morning, Ellis. I hope you don't mind me popping over, I was a little worried when your new barista whispered you were at the station.'

Ellis told the young man with him to head back to Dukes. He would be over soon.

'Remember, not a word to anyone about what we discussed in our meeting. Can I trust you on that?'

His barista nodded and scuttled off.

Ellis put his fingers through his thinning hair and sighed.

'What's going on, Ellis? How can I help?'

'I don't know. All that came up was that Jake,' he pointed after his departing barista, 'saw two girls taking the bus across at the stop in front of Dukes during his dawn shift. I had to get him here to report what he saw.'

'Really? That's a good lead, right?'

'All he saw was two of them hop onto the bus at Illyria Square, twenty minutes apart. He thought nothing of it until he overheard me speaking to you yesterday morning. But the idiot only called me late last night when the information made him sleepless.'

'You can't blame him. Nobody expects anything sinister to happen in Blackwater Ridge. Did he say precisely what time he saw them get onto the bus?'

'Five-fifteen, and around five thirty-five.'

'Who are the two girls he saw.'

'Milsom's granddaughter and the neighbor's boarder, I think.'

'Let me know how I can help.'

Ellis took another deep, long breath.

'I don't think there's much we can do but wait. It's a police case, now.'

As much as she hated to admit it. There was nothing they could do.

Somehow the news had spread overnight. Almost fifty percent of the student population were absent at the Academy. Viola's red-faced assistant fielded calls from parents wanting homework to be emailed to their children. A strange mood prevailed over the Academy, each lost in their thoughts.

The mayor's office called to invite Viola to a select emergency meeting at 7pm in the town hall on Broaden Parade.

Viola walked via the beach to the meeting. Ellis took a roll call as each invitee entered the hall.

Heads of six organizations were in attendance. And Viola pondered why she received an invitation when she saw Andy in conversation with the police commissioner and church priest. Andy took half days off from teaching this week to assist his wife and her brother during this trying time.

The mayor called the room to order.

'Respected leaders, thank you for your presence here tonight. And at short notice. We need to put our thinking caps on for a way forward in this situation that has arisen.'

It amazed Viola to note the townsfolk's inability to call it what it was without skirting around matters. The priest sat behind the mayor with palms together throughout his address. The mayor added that *this matter* had to resolved *within* the Blackwater community.

'I do not want to make this a nationwide issue and appeal for your silence in withholding anything discussed here. It is not to be taken outside this forum.'

Different scenarios played out as Viola listened without missing a beat. There was no word on whether Andy's wife's niece alighted the bus at Illyria Square. Was this a prank? Did the girls run off to meet secret lovers? Did they plan together to leave as they did? Milsom's granddaughter was a newcomer, and she struggled with anxiety and depression.

The mayor praised Ellis' barista, Jake, for speaking up on what he observed during his early morning shift at Dukes.

'I suggest we check with the bus driver on whether he observed anything out of the ordinary when the young women alighted his bus.'

Viola raised her hand.

'Questions, at the end, Ms Bardo.'

'A quick question, Mayor Corey,' she appealed.

'What is it, Ms Bardo?'

Mayor Corey's raised eyebrows ironed out the wrinkles around his sagging eyes.

'With due respect, Mayor Corey, aren't we wasting time talking and surmising when we should be door knocking for leads? The people are the eyes and ears of what goes on in the town. If probed, they will speak up.'

'I understand your point, Ms Bardo, but the occurrence has spooked the folk, and I have a duty and obligation as mayor of this town to keep things calm.'

Sweat popped on Viola's brow. This was not the time to pussyfoot around not alarming the townsfolk. Danger was two days old, and something had to be done!

All she could do was say what she had to say. Anything more bordered on insubordination in this forum.

Then Ellis spoke up.

'Corey, it would be wise to send some of us into the community. We can quell fears and let our people know it is part of their civic duty to report what they know that might hurt our town.'

Mayor Corey fixed a hard gaze on Ellis.

'Look Ellis, we should be able to glean some information from the bus driver before we create a disturbance by poking around too much.'

Nothing and no one could deter Mayor Corey from losing control over the town's actions. Dare Viola say it – power and politics, and personal agendas! What he failed to admit was that he had no control over the girls leaving.

Andy was antsy, and Viola had the urge to ask if any news surfaced on whether his wife's niece also caught the bus later that morning. Andy jumped to his feet.

'I am going on that bus route in search of answers. I cannot sit here and hope the young women will turn up. They are our daughters, siblings, nieces, and friends. To do nothing, to preserve the privacy of the town, is sacrilege!'

He strode out the town hall door, leaving a stunned audience behind him.

Nobody moved a muscle until the police commissioner declared the meeting closed.

Nothing made sense by the end of the meeting. Viola knew a call to Sebastian would help clear the muddiness.

8

Mayor Corey faced his first challenge after forty years. Nobody questioned his authority or decisions. His deadweight leadership had all but paused the town hall clock. Now two of the town's respected men, Ellis and Andy, spoke their minds on the *issue*.

None of the missing young women's families were present at the meeting. Andy was the only relative of his wife's niece. Milsom, a founding father of the town, was ignored. Perhaps to spare him emotional despair. Viola knew Milsom to be a level-headed man.

She called Sebastian for a neutral perspective into the situation. Matthew had slipped into the background and talking to him might give her father false hope since the two were bosom buddies after Matthew's trip to Portugal.

Sebastian picked up her call just as she was about to end the persistent ringing. His voice said it all. He had man flu. She saw its crippling effect on him when they worked together in Athens.

'I apologize for taking so long to answer your call,' he sniffed. 'HR ordered me to stay home as it's a severe strain of the flu and my students are at risk before their exam.'

'I'm sorry that you are unwell. My father would order you a brandy and honey, or rather mix you one himself. He has a heavy hand on the brandy!'

Sebastian tried to laugh, 'Your father sounds like my kind of man.'

She wondered whether Sebastian's flu was stress induced. He had a puppy to look after and was drowning with grading papers with larger classes at the university.

'This is probably not a good time to talk on matters that need your clarity.'

'I'm not on my death bed, so go ahead say it. I'm listening.'

Viola summed up what had happened in the town, avoiding any deliberations that would tire Sebastian.

After a few snuffling sounds, he cleared his throat.

'This is a police matter.'

'As are all the cases we have worked on together and those that I worked on alone.'

'I sense your itch to be involved but your leadership role at the Academy makes it impossible.'

'Itch? No. Doing the right thing while the mayor dances with danger, looking after the town's good name at the sacrifice of the safety of the young women. I think it is essential that an investigation happens now, but agree that in my present role I do not have the physical time available to investigate.'

The pause that followed heightened the sound of Sebastian's heavy breathing.

'Here's the thing, if I were in your position, I would hand it over to Tempest. That is what you would have me do, right?'

'Yes, please, but as you are unwell, I can send Tempest an email and wait out her reply although time is of the essence.'

Professionalism came first to Viola, and Sebastian had time to learn that about her during the Athens' case. She had to serve justice, but now as Rob Dwyer's acting principal, she had to keep her eye on the campus. Sebastian set up a conference call with Tempest and asked to be excused from speaking because of his hacking cough.

Tempest set the call outside of Viola's Academy working hours.

* * *

Tempest's husky voice was a welcome soother. Sebastian whispered his greeting to alert Viola to his presence.

'Good evening, Viola, or should I say, agent Bardo, trouble follows you wherever you go. I am sorry to hear that young women have disappeared in Blackwater Ridge.'

'Thank you so much for calling, Tempest. The town is in a quandary on where to begin and there is the old school thinking churning in the background about keeping the secret within the town.'

'Hmmm… Sebastian says the barista at Dukes saw the young women leaving on the bus. Is that correct?'

'Yes, he noted two leaving but the third is a mystery.'

'I could get my contacts onto this right away as every minute wasted pontificating the rights and wrongs could cost a life. Your one-man police department needs help on this.'

'I agree but can guarantee that help will not be appreciated. It might be construed as a takeover or as showing up the incompetence of the town's leadership.'

'I meant a clandestine operation as we do with our other cases, just without your active involvement. I get the small-town secrecy and family-oriented community. I grew up in a town much like Blackwater Ridge.'

It surprised Viola to hear Tempest drop the first ever piece of autobiographical information.

'I trust your judgement with confidence. This is the way to go. Finding the young women is necessary for their families and not a time to value power over their protection.'

'I will put some probes in place but as always cannot guarantee the answer we most want. And I know you cannot be an active participant but the eyes and ears to pass on anything unusual is all we ask of you.'

Before Viola could thank Tempest for her intuition and candor, she was gone.

'Sebastian, you still on the line?'

'Yes, Viola, I am.'

'Gosh, you were awfully quiet.'

'I was just the messenger and wanted you two to have the space to talk about the best approach. I used my coughing as an excuse for my silence. It is a unique situation with you being professionally prohibited from embroiling yourself in the case. A little different to how far you could get involved with the *Galleria Bardo* case.'

Viola had no option. She had to get involved when the night wanderer she named Mural Man appeared whenever she entered the mural laneways in Porto.

'I am glad that you are letting Tempest spin some magic dust on this. I chose to be quiet. Lord knows I have had my fair share of chastisements for butting in at the wrong moment.'

This lightened the mood as both laughed over Sebastian's dog-box moments for his overzealous questions and outbursts.

'Between you and me, I think Tempest is unwell. When I called her, she had a coughing fit and had to call me back.'

'Really? I have noticed nothing, except that her voice is deeper, sort of mellow and yet rough, if you know what I mean.'

'I do. It exhausted her when we spoke and she said she had not had a good night's sleep.'

'Hmmm... yes, she dropped a personal bit about growing up in a small town. Now, that is a first for her. I feel guilty for allowing her to proceed with this.'

'It's her life's work so whether you agreed or disagreed she will do what she has to do.'

'Let us watch the situation and I might ask if I hear her coughing. She strikes me as a lonely soul.'

'Rather you, than me, I'm not going there with Tempest. Her bite hurts. And aren't we all lonely souls when we want to instil joy in others?'

They parted as good friends softened by the pain of their significant ally.

* * *

TEMPEST OPENED the balcony door to energize her aching spirit and joints. She coughed again after almost five years of peaceful sleep and no cough medicine. Her specialist advised that she moved into town to have the hospital facilities nearby. Tempest refused. She needed the solitude of the lonely house above the vast sand dunes overlooking the sea. Life was whatever it was at any and every point of living. She had no control of what lay ahead. Expiry was beyond human control. John Donne accepted that in his tussle with life and death. If life was a library card, then free will kicked in on when to check out and in. It was not to be. The *Librarian,* the wise woman in the sky, had the final say when the expiration date was up on who she would pluck out of existence. Such was the book of life.

She needed her pipe now and stepped back inside. The addiction had to stop, but that was one small pleasure she would not forgo. Khaya and Woza whimpered at her feet when they sensed her restless spirit. Both slept at the foot of her bed when the coughing overpowered her. They fixed their doleful eyes on her with ears pricked at every sound of her raspy cough. Khaya dragged Tempest's slippers around wherever she walked. Her swelling feet avoided shoes and being barefooted all day calloused and cracked her heels. She lacked energy to take care of her physical appearance. Once, this was her pride, dressed in the finery of the African continent, beads and earrings the color of the earth, sarongs and kaftans emblazoned in the orange of a setting sun.

She picked up her apple and maple pipe and drew back long and hard. A fit of coughs had Khaya and Woza skating towards her reading chair, helpless, listening to their beloved Mama Tempest struggle for air. When she recovered, she looked at her only companions.

'Quit those scolding eyes. I will be here for a while longer than you think. I have unfinished business.'

She tossed them a treat each and slumped back in her seat, exhausted. Her agents Sebastian and Viola worked well together and soon would not need much intervention from her. She had to set things up for their solo run as agents. Viola, she knew had a good head on her shoulders. She thought things through before acting. It was Sebastian who needed more guidance, but his potential was vast. Both her agents combined were a lethal cocktail against injustice. The Blackwater Ridge missing girls needed her full attention. Tempest reached for her journal on her side table and scribbled down her plan. One thing she was sure about was that Sebastian had to go to Blackwater Ridge to be her agent on the ground. Viola's acting principalship left her no time for an investigation. Sebastian had a way of warming himself into people's hearts. The town needed someone like him to guide them out of this worrying secret situation.

The second thing that needed her attention was her succession plan. The Lady in the sky would not hold out forever.

9

Andy and Fabian set out on the bus route without the blessings from the mayor and the police commissioner. The bus driver's identity was withheld, making Andy's task difficult in tracking down where the young women disembarked on the town circle route. All he knew was that Nadia, Milsom's granddaughter, left home wearing a black tracksuit and red runners.

Viola was the only other person privy to their secret bus route investigation. Both men alighted the bus in Illyria Square, across from Dukes at the same time the barista noted the departure of the first young woman, Milsom's granddaughter.

Mayor Corey clung to his power, afraid to lose control to two school teachers almost half his age. His tenacity reeked of insecurity. Everybody knew he was losing his grip on decision making. Yet nobody spoke up or encouraged him to step down from the role. It was as though the seat was one, he would die in. He kept the town where it was for four decades. Time and progress stood still when the mine shut down.

Andy's pressure came from his family's angst when his wife's niece, Vivian, disappeared with no sighting of her having

50

boarded the bus that morning. Fabian's loyalty to his friend made him join Andy's private search. He was an unrelenting adherent for social justice. Wrongs had to be righted regardless of the price sacrificed. Reprimanding the intern, Charlotte Ainsworth would have cost him his job, or a period of suspension, had the board presided over the matter.

That Saturday morning armed with backpacks loaded with water, a few dry snacks and a change of wet gear clothes, they left, determined that if it took the entire weekend to gain a lead or two, they were in for it. The search at the first town circle stop yielded nothing. They got off at Adriatic Park, the second stop, and walked into the park. After a hurried toilet stop they split up to search opposite ends of the park. Andy went north and Fabian south.

Andy lifted fallen leaves and branches and poked around every shrub until he found a red and black scarf. A quick photograph to his wife confirmed it was Vivian's. This was a breakthrough find that she had indeed boarded the bus. The bus driver knew something and had to be found.

'This is Vivian's scarf. My wife ticked that box. Our suspicion is confirmed, the three young women are on the same mission.'

'Bag the scarf, here, I have a zip-lock bag, and a permanent marker.'

'Wow! You're like a seasoned forensics man.'

'Comes from watching too many television crime shows!'

'Vivian must be somewhere close. We should continue searching.'

'I hate to sound like a fatalist, but if she is nearby, she would have come looking for her scarf.'

'Point noted,' a disappointed Andy sighed, 'let's get back onto the bus when it returns and goes through to the next stop. We can ask this driver if he was on a shift on that dreadful day.'

'I doubt he will know anything, he's a casual driver and has no interest in what goes on in the town.'

'I will ask.' Andy stretched himself out on a bench and closed his eyes. Few people walked in the park today.

One lone woman pushed a stroller and paid no attention to their presence.

Fabian huddled crossed legged on the grass, scribbling in their findings and his speculations. They appeared hapless and homeless, out of the comfort zone of their classrooms.

Dark clouds brewed overhead and a gust of wind rolled into the park. Andy jumped to his feet.

'We should get to the third stop before rain impedes our search. Those clouds look determined! Thank you for helping me out, Fabian.'

Andy patted Fabian's shoulder in gratitude for his company, for being his eyes, ears and thinking.

'You would do the same for me, no sweat mate!'

Like clockwork the bus returned on its town circle round.

The driver was a different man. Something both Andy and Fabian did not expect.

'Clay, how come you're on this round. Where is the other driver?'

'Not happy to see me, Andy? Sorry to disappoint!' Clay laughed and coughed at the same time.

'You are just the person we need to see.'

Clay looked from Andy's face to Fabian's.

'What's happening? You boys not going home today? Escaping domestic chores, are you? Is it a boys' weekend out?'

His wheezy laugh released the tension Andy felt. Clay smoked more than he ate or drank. His cough spoke of an unwell man.

Clay took voluntary semi-retirement six months ago, a range of casual drivers took over his full-time town circuit run.

Mayor Corey ran everything down to who drove the bus around town.

'Nah, not a boy's weekend at all. Do you remember any of the missing young women getting off at this stop?'

Clay's reaction was quick.

'Nope, sorry Andy. I know your wife's niece is missing and you and the family are worried sick. I was off at the doctor's that morning. Saw nothing, I'm afraid.'

Nobody mentioned publicly who Vivian was. How did Clay know this detail?

'Who took over from you that day? We need to speak to him, urgently.'

'Not sure off the top of my head. I'll check my roster and let you know when I get home.'

Andy mentioned the day and time to jog Clay's memory.

'Look, it might have been Zac, but I can't say for sure.'

'Why don't you call him now to verify?'

'Can't do that. Zac is on a week's leave, and out-of-town on some family matter. We had a casual driver today, but he can't cope with a full day. Mayor asked me to pick up the shift. I'm on overload but can't refuse Mayor Corey. He does so much for us.'

There was no point in forcing a Corey fan to speak up.

'Thanks Clay, we will head to the next stop and get off. We'll catch you on the return round.'

'Righty-o, but remember, the run stops at 6 pm and picks up again at 5 am tomorrow.'

Andy and Fabian got off the bus and waited until Clay disappeared round the corner.

'Clay's too nice a guy to be lying, right?' Fabian probed.

'Lying about Zac?'

'Not just that but everything.'

'I don't think he would, but I stand to be corrected.'

They wandered around the streets until they came across the milk-bar.

Fabian went over to ask a few questions and returned ten minutes later.

'The owner says he saw no girls, and that Zac came in for a coffee and a pack of ciggies.'

'Is Clay's memory foggy or is he shielding Zac for some reason.'

Clay picked Andy and Fabian up on the return journey.

'Any luck gentlemen?'

'Nothing.'

'Never you worry. Mayor Corey will sort this out. And the girls will be home in no time.'

'Yeah, true,' Andy lied, shooting Fabian a dubious look.

Everyday lost in finding the young women increased the risk of something terrible happening to them.

* * *

BACK IN TOWN Viola was in a tizzy with Andy's news that Vivian's scarf surfaced in Adriatic Park. Perhaps she headed off somewhere on foot. The whispering thoughts of someone having enticed her or followed her out of the park had to be shut down. She wanted to be involved in the hunt for the young women.

Tempest spoke to Sebastian about flying to Blackwater Ridge.

'Do you have outstanding leave that you can take now, right now?'

'No ma'am, I don't have any leave days due.'

'I suggest you take some *family crisis* leave and get to Blackwater Ridge to assist.'

'When would you have me do this?'

'Yesterday, if I had my way. I have your ticket booked. Get out by tomorrow. Wrap up things at work. It will be unpaid leave. I have your finances covered.'

'It's short notice, but I will process the online application today. It takes about forty-eight hours to be cleared.'

'Cleared or not, go!'

'Aye, aye captain, got it!'

'Tempest, not, captain, got that, boy!'

Sebastian froze when Tempest's hacking cough followed her angry outburst. He waited for her to leave the conversation and found all required travel documents in his inbox. As always, Tempest was one step ahead. He submitted his leave application, called the puppy pound to take care of Jasper, tossed some clothes and his passport into a small bag. Tempest's unexpected request and reaction caught Sebastian off guard.

When human lives were in jeopardy, Tempest pushed all buttons, doing whatever was possible to get the wheels of justice in motion. All Sebastian had to do was step up when called.

Deep down, he knew the university could terminate his contract because of his frequent requests for leave.

10

Viola had the urge to do the Adumu, Maasai dance when she heard Sebastian was on his way to Blackwater Ridge. It was the rain she needed in the aridity of her acting position, tied to expectations and protocol. Taking on the position, was her expression of respect for Rob Dwyer. This town cried out for fresh blood. The lack of growth in the leadership was becoming obvious to her as each new situation arose. Something she had never confronted before. Up close, it made her uncomfortable that Mayor Corey and his police commissioner ignored the urgency of attention the situation needed.

Too laid back.

Too closed.

Secretive.

Not good for anyone!

TEMPEST LEFT Sebastian to explain when he would arrive, and what she expected him to do. The elusive Tempest triggered the action and sat in the wings, watching her plan unfold. She had

profound respect for her agents. Sebastian was a little rough
around the edges as an investigator, but he was a fast learner.
Tempest never left her agents in the lurch. She observed from
afar, like a lioness watching her cubs, stepping in only when
needed.

Sebastian's joy was infectious.

'We are destined to meet again, so soon. Porto was a temporary physical separation.'

'Indeed, we are, number two, although I'm not sure if
Tempest has moved me to number two and you as her number
one agent. Either way, I'm so pleased you're heading my way.'

'You do know we have to maintain minimum contact, right?
So, no pizza and pistachio ice cream jaunts like we did in
Athens.'

'Yes, I know. Where will you be staying, and for how long?
Am I allowed to know?'

'You will know everything. I don't intend leaving you in the
dark. I am booked at a bedsitter near the beach to be away from
the town center and the temptation to pop in to see you at the
Academy. I can't afford any wrist slapping from Tempest again.
She's on edge these days.'

'She has great faith in what you can achieve, as do I.'

'Thank you kindly, agent Bardo! I am expected to maintain a
good relationship with your local police department and work
with them.'

'Not much of a department, I'm afraid. Just one police
commissioner, so you will have your work cut out for you.'

'I had a feeling it was understaffed. But this is grossly understaffed!'

'Tempest knows how small-town talk can ruin a case. She is
right about us maintaining distance when you assist with the
case. Let me know when you arrive. I feel awful that I can't meet
you at the airport and drive you over.'

'I will be in touch. Who knows, we might be able to meet in person.'

'Don't take a chance, Sebastian. Tempest will know your every move. Leave the arrangement as it is and let's see how it goes.'

'You will know I'm around, never you mind.'

'Cryptic! Please, not another Mural Man in my life. I do not want any surprises. Let's march on with things as they are.'

'For now, I agree. *See* you in Oz!'

ANDY CALLED Viola around 7 am on Sunday morning to brief her on all his and Fabian's findings during their bus route check. He needed advice on whether to hand over Vivian's scarf to the police commissioner. It was a Catch-22 situation, the emotional sentiment of the scarf to his brother-in-law's family and doing the right thing as an upstanding citizen of Blackwater Ridge. The inertia of Mayor Corey's leadership worried him. Viola's own leadership role compromised the level of advice she could offer Andy. Blackwater Ridge Academy had to be uppermost in all she said and did. As a leader in the town, she could not openly berate the soft touch of the mayorship.

The missing young women were never students of the Academy, but her allegiance was to assist in having them safely returned to their families. In a small town such as Blackwater Ridge, leaders of all sectors, education, health, business, and others had to pull together. Advice dispensed without thought could come back to bite her. Human nature was fickle at the best of times, and more so now in pitting its wits against an establishment such as Mayor Corey's tiny old office.

'Look Andy, all I can offer is that you do what your head and heart see fit to bring you and your wife's family peace.'

In the moment of that conversation, Viola felt the gravitas of

Rob's role – leader and elder as a long-standing member of the town's community. It did not always go as he hoped it would. He kept his opinions private on the town's management. His focus was to allow students to grow in their own light without hemming them into the shadows of old thinking. Freedom of speech meant everything to him. He lived that value with no qualms. Hurt by verbal attacks from disgruntled staff, vulnerability sought refuge in his office until the storm passed. Confrontation was not Rob's way.

Andy, trapped between ethics and family favor, had nothing more to say.

Mayor Corey and the police commissioner held him in high esteem, and both expected the same respect.

Now the town's waters were churning.

Viola lay in bed for an hour after Andy's call, mulling over the direction he would choose. His unhappiness apparent in his bruised tone that she could not give him a clear directive on how to proceed. She dragged her poetry journal out of her bedside draw, in need of her own clarity.

> *what's ego, pride and power*
> *lives are in danger*
> *and fresh wounds open*
> *butting against old blood...*

THAT SEEMED ENOUGH FOR NOW. Viola hit a wall. In those lines lay the rub of the matter. She went out to the beach to clear her tangled thoughts and stopped at Dukes for a coffee. Ellis was alone in this strangely deserted popular haunt in Blackwater Ridge.

'Morning Ellis, how are you?'

'Viola! Glad somebody showed up this morning. It sure is an eerie morning.'

'Where's everyone?'

'The folk are tense, with no news on the young women yet. I suppose they feel they don't want to hear bad news.'

'It won't come to that.'

Ellis wondered what Viola knew.

'Do you think the caravanners might know or have seen something untoward the morning the women disappeared?'

'I doubt it. They do not get involved in the daily goings on around here. They come in like a whirlwind and leave but with no disturbance.'

Two patrons staggered in for coffee, hung over from a rough night.

Viola slipped out with a quick wave to Ellis. Body odor lingered in the air making her lightheaded.

Walking helped process doubts. She was sure Ellis was not partisan to Mayor Corey's style of governance. Once the thought entered her head, she was not sure anymore. Politics was a shady business. Back-stabbing in government was a known practice. She wished she could sound her thoughts with Rob. He was recuperating at home, but under strict instructions not to have visitors just yet.

She had a sugar craving that she thought she had overcome, but found the strength to ignore it today. This craving lasted for a brief spell and thankfully left no headache. Sometimes her migraine lingered for almost three days. She opted to get her paperwork done to have a free afternoon to read. A batch of scones baked for her staff morning tea relaxed her. She was due for a medical check-up after her dizzy spells increased in Porto. Now was not the right time.

Thoughts of Matthew returned after she had put him on hold. He was giving her the space she asked for. There was no call from him since her return. They had come close to declaring their hearts to each other after a few intimate moments, one that the scallywag Alonso ruined for them. Intimacy broke the ice, but commitment was a steel wall around her heart. She knew she pushed him away when they left Porto, and guilt crept in that he might think she used him to get her father out of a mess he did not create. Listlessness set her on the path to her past, where much remained unresolved.

No closure on Lorenza's disappearance.

Her motor vehicle accident and the trauma that followed on not having the nerve to drive again. Writing helped ease the torment of those days. Now disturbed by the lack of urgency that three young women were missing in Blackwater Ridge, and she did not have the freedom to intervene.

She flipped open her laptop and drafted an email to Matthew Soto.

My dearest Matthew,

This must come as a surprise. I think of you warmly and our days in Porto often. I hope this finds you and Jungen well. Papa says you will spend Easter at Galleria Bardo. How wonderful! I am happy you and papa have grown close. So much is going on here. It seems I attract trouble wherever I go. This time it's not personal, but I am a Blackwater Ridge citizen now and feel its angst deeply.

Enough of me. Do write and tell me how you and Jungen are. I will call papa over the Easter weekend and might have a chat with you then. Stay well. Viola.

She hovered over the send button for a minute and hit delete instead. He would have to make the first move. There was much that needed her rational eye and mind now.

A message from Ellis that a city newspaper journalist had

taken up residence in a motel close to Illyria Square would send the already anxious townsfolk into deeper hibernation.

11

An outsider on a one-man mission with a large camera strapped to his shoulders set his prying eyes on Blackwater Ridge, sending the mayor and police commissioner into a neurotic state.

A letter box drop went out in a blitz informing residents to avoid all strangers, and to stay indoors as far as possible, stepping out only for essentials.

The town with its shutters down went into a lockdown.

The media stranger, an enemy of the town, demonized by leaders. An *innocent* town reacting this way had Viola wondering what secrets lay concealed in the mayor's residence. She fought the temptation to eat the last surviving scone from the batch she baked for her staff, on Sunday. Restlessness craved forbidden treats. Staff devoured most of the scones with a grateful heart. Her dizzy spells had stopped, but a niggling voice nudged her to book an appointment with the local GP, Dr Burrows. His rooms were two doors down from Dukes. Traveling on foot made Blackwater Ridge an easy access town with essential services huddled in one location. Dr Burrows asked her to pop in by 7 am for a blood test before his consultation. Her morning coffee and catch up with Ellis had to be delayed.

She slipped into easy fit pants, a creaseless white blouse, and a pair of black pumps before she whisked down to Dr Burrows rooms.

It was a crisp morning at this time of year. Summer mornings could be like midday heat in the tropics. Today it felt like spring. Summer paused, building up its intensity. As Viola turned the corner into Illyria Square, she stopped at the top to relish the view of the ocean from that height. The waves lapped onto the shore like a playful kitten. She loved living here. Amid the noise and uneasiness of now, nature never failed to inspire.

Dr Burrows let her in at 6:55 am playing receptionist until his staff arrived at 9 am.

'Good to see you, Ms Bardo. How are things at Blackwater Ridge Performing Arts Academy without Rob?'

'Going well, thank you, but I miss not having Rob around.'

'Let me prick your arm, then. Your results will return in a week. The day we have our own Blackwater Ridge laboratory, things will move a lot faster around here.'

Viola rolled up her sleeve and made a fist as Dr Burrows instructed.

'Dear, dear, dear, you have fine, spider veins. Keep pumping your fists in quick tight bursts.'

Like Mayor Corey, Dr Burrows was pushing past his mid-seventies. He panted, exhausted, from trying to get Viola's veins to pop. As he pulled away, blood squirted across her white blouse.

'I'm sorry about that, Ms Bardo. I hope you brought along a change of clothes. I have enough in this vial now. You should get your coffee and be sure to drink a glass or two of water – coffee steals your calcium. I know you teachers cannot start your day without coffee.'

Viola chuckled. 'You have extracted a vial of coffee from me. I hope you know that!'

'Off you go then into your busy day.'

Dr Burrows was another grand old gentleman in the town.

* * *

A GRAY BEARDED man sat reading the newspaper at Dukes. She stopped at the entrance – her cheerful greeting evaporated when she caught Ellis' warning look. He raised his hand in acknowledgment of her entry, and she did the same. He rolled his eyes in referral to the silent patron, sipping his coffee without looking up.

When she got close to the counter Ellis mouthed, *media.*

She nodded.

'How are you, Ms Bardo? A lovely fresh morning promises a beautiful day, a pity you will be in your office all day. We need more days like this.'

'I'm good, thank you, Ellis. It is quite lovely out there. I need my coffee to go, please? I could stay here all day!'

Small talk, stifled this morning by the eyes and ears of a stranger in their midst, ended Viola's usual morning chit-chat stop at Dukes. The stranger's eyes lifted to follow her exit.

* * *

NOTHING ELSE SEEMED unusual on this Tuesday. Many students stayed at home after the letter box drop from the mayor's office. School seemed to be excluded by some families, made a non-essential. Mayor Corey called off all meetings using Ellis as his messenger should something significant come up on the missing young women. Ellis set up the leadership advisory committee and gave Viola no room to opt out.

She walked through a deserted town on her way home that

afternoon. The Academy shut an hour earlier because many teachers and students took the day off. This afternoon she bypassed Dukes and headed home to prepare a grilled chicken breast meal with steamed vegetables. A glass of red was necessary, and *me* time an unprescribed essential. She heard her phone ping in her handbag as she busied herself preparing dinner. When she finally reached for her phone, there were several messages from her mother.

Where are you? Can you talk now?
Let me know the best time to call you.

She called her mother.

Conversation was never part of their relationship.

'Hello mother, how are you?'

'Well, as expected. I understand how busy you are, but surely you can give up some time to call me. It's been ages since I last heard a squeak from you.'

Viola's childhood hit her across the head with that comment. A squeak was all her mother thought of her. It silenced her then.

Not anymore…

'Yes, it has been busy with this leadership role. Unlike you, I was not born to lead, as you know. I am finding my way though.'

'Tut! Tut! No need to be touchy, now! I spoke to your father. Have you been in touch with him? Do you know what's going on in his world?'

'He calls and texts often. Why, what seems to be the problem?'

'Your father has two unknown entities living with him at his gallery home. One he calls 'Ariel,' and the other, 'Matt'. One would think he would be careful after that hullabaloo over Christmas.'

'Papa knows what he's doing. I know the people you refer to. He's not the naive husband you divorced.'

Her mother laughed like a vexatious vixen ready to attack at every move.

'You could have fooled me, but then again you do not understand how easily swayed he is.'

'That is an outdated thought, mother.'

Viola's anger rose. She knew she had to stop before she said something she would regret later.

'Who are these people living in his house?'

Silence.

'Who are they, Viola? Answer me, please.'

Helena's claim to politeness vanished when she was woman desperate to know her ex-husband's business. Viola believed she still cared but was too arrogant to admit it to Placido.

'Ariel is like family to papa, and Matthew is a friend of mine. He has great respect and admiration for papa.'

Viola heard her mother's deep sigh and unexpected subdued response.

'I see. If you say so.'

The conversation dried to an inconsistent drip from that point. Viola filled the silence with an explanation on why she preferred to be a classroom teacher and that leadership was not her goal.

They parted with a terse goodbye, with neither angered by how it ended.

VIOLA'S unshakeable irritation was why had Matthew neglected to tell her he was with her father, long before his planned Easter trip. The temptation to call her father, halted her in a self-check moment by what she had said to her mother. Her father did indeed know what he was doing. He did not need a daughter and meddlesome ex-wife watching his every move. But she was restless.

Her parents married in the haste of first attraction, and led a carefree nomadic life traveling and living for brief spells in several parts of the world until she was born in Mozambique. The union ended leaving Placido pining for his wife for years after she had walked out on him. Her mother's infidelity broke their family. He was not a quarrelsome man, and her mother's fiery nature and adventurous spirit detested her father's contemplative years. She fell in love with her once impulsive artist husband, not the man who desired solitude. People grew apart later in life, an older, wiser Viola accepted, and to stay in a toxic relationship harmed everyone in the union. The bald fact of the matter was that her mother had to have her way.

Thoughts drifted to Sebastian and Matthew. They too had fractured childhoods. Matthew was comfortable with who he was. The need to find his roots, consumed Sebastian. His childhood, a lived scar under his skin. That his mother gave him up at birth contributed to this need for perfection.

Nobody was free from a tangled past.

Imperfection dwells in all souls, it is the stuff that builds character, to be a person for others.

12

Sebastian arrived in Blackwater Ridge on a gloomy Thursday afternoon. High winds whisked his cap clean off his head as he exited the taxi. He watched it float off like a kite. He figured while he was in Blackwater Ridge, he would wear a cap to conceal his identity to protect Viola – by some stroke of luck, by Tempest's decree, they might meet somewhere under public gaze.

His message to Viola read:

The eagle has landed in gale force winds. Happy to report my feathers are intact! Call you tonight.

Several meetings with parents voicing their concerns on matters of their daughters' safety preoccupied her day. At 4:30 pm she kicked off her shoes, exhausted from the energy drained by each meeting. Parents had a right to be concerned, she increased security around the Academy, and students' mental wellness took priority during this time of fear and uncertainty.

Sebastian's message comforted her in knowing he was a short walk away, although Tempest prohibited any meetups. They had to lie low as vigilante investigators with Viola as a silent partner. Any whiff that they were vigilante agents would invite the same hostility the media received.

Two weeks and no news on the missing young women, escalated Viola's anxiety. The worst scenario she had trouble dismissing was the horror of human trafficking. The police commissioner continued to work alone – nothing changed.

Sebastian was the hope the town needed.

Her first call at the close of her working day was to her father. She needed his calm spirit.

'*Galleria Bardo*, how may I help you?'

Viola paused when a familiar voice sent her into a flutter.

'Matthew?'

'Oh! Hello Viola, It must be a surprise to know I'm here with your father.'

She bit her lip, accepting that he was visiting her father. That he was there before Easter, with no word to her, and her mother knew before she did, annoyed her.

'It certainly is a surprise. Papa said nothing about your arrival.'

'He was just as surprised when I called him from the Pestana to tell him I was back. And your father, the generous man he is, insisted Jungen and I stay with him while we are here. I checked out of the hotel yesterday and came over.'

'I'm glad you're keeping papa company. He'll relish having you there. How is Jungen?'

'He's good but asks when you will be back.'

Matthew, transparent as ever, used Jungen to convey his heart's questions. When she left Porto saying she did not want commitment, he accepted her wish without a fuss or appeal for consideration. This irritated her, hurt her, yet she said it to protect herself from the intensity she felt for him. Her watertight decision never to give her heart away was challenged. He was too much like her.

'Give Jungen, my love. I will call another day to talk to him.

May I speak to my father, please? Lovely to chat with you again.'

Matthew's silence and whispered, 'Sure,' conveyed her officious manner stung him. He did not know how many nights she lay awake, longing to be in his arms, feeling his caress and tenderness. His voice excited her like no other, and that scared her. He would never know her secret longing. Their budding romance in Porto emerged when she was most vulnerable. Now she was strong at defending and protecting her heart. He put his life on the line for her, and for that she was grateful. Guilt caught her in that thought, she called out, 'Speak to me for a while...' She heard her father panting as he shuffled to the telephone.

'Artista! This is a pleasant surprise.'

'Hello papa. I called first, this time. Enjoy your days with Jungen and Matthew.'

Her father sensed the little girl surfacing, jealous that she was missing out.

'It would have been wonderful if you were here with us, meu filho.'

That was enough to warm her.

'I wish I were there, too. So, what are you getting up to while I'm away?' She laughed.

'Jungen has me on my toes, so he's keeping me young.'

'That's good, you're getting in some exercise! Mother called me after a long time.'

'Oh? She is doing her yearly rounds because she called me a day ago asking if I had heard from you.'

'Yeah, more her curiosity about what you're up to.'

'Really? She spoke to me for all of five minutes, so what's that about?'

'She loves *knowing* all things *Placido* and quizzed me about Ariel and Matthew being at the house with you.'

Placido's chesty laugh, and mellow tones filled Viola's ears. Her father's mirth was contagious.

'Ah, so you knew Matthew was here. Is that why you called today without a message first? Curiosity will never kill Helena, and how about you, my kitten?'

Viola felt injured by that judgement, but her papa's hearty laugh, and coughing fit, softened her hurt.

'Helena still loves *you*, is what *I* think.'

'Don't be silly. She walked away from me. Cheated with another man and married him. Bah! Some strange love, if that.'

'She will hang on to you, because it hurts her more not knowing what you're doing with your life.'

'Perhaps I should spice it up. Tell her I have an exotic new love and then see what she says.'

'Now, now, don't be naughty. It does not become you. I'll leave you to enjoy your house guests and call you once they've left.'

'Would you like to chat to Matthew again?'

'Another day, perhaps papa. I have a few things to attend to before I sleep tonight.'

'Don't work too hard, meu filho. Chat again soon. Love you.'

VIOLA HAD a pile of work to get through before she could rest her weary head. She imagined moving over to Porto to live with her father, in a permanent capacity, but had to see through this temporary role. The jarring buzz of the cell phone intruded into her imagination.

'Hey, Viola, no welcome mat for me!' Sebastian bellowed into her ear.

'Sebastian, welcome to Oz! How are you?'

'I'm well but worried when you did not reply to my message.'

'I replied at 4:30 pm, it has been such a crazy day.'

'Nope, no message from you. Did you reply to the number I sent my message from? I have a new temporary OZ number.'

'Hang on a sec, let me check.'

'Oh, don't worry.'

Viola clicked back on her messages.

'Oh no! Sebastian I am so sorry, the typed message is unsent from my end. Something must have grabbed my attention. Like I said, this has been a mad day. I'm so sorry.'

'No worries, mate. He laughed, 'I'm learning the lingo, already!'

'Be careful, once imbibed, you can never lose it! Have you had news from Tempest? I haven't had any contact, but that's my fault for being bogged in a ton of work and the stress of everything that's going on.'

'Tempest's last conversation before I left New York was to change my number each time I contacted you. She wants nothing to be tracked to you. I feel it in my gut that something is going on in her life. Perhaps she has fallen in love.'

'Stop that! Tempest married justice, moons ago. She is a generous, kind soul. I hope she's not unwell, but we will never know unless she tells us so. Rest and I'll send you the police commissioner's details. I think you should mosey over to Dukes and introduce yourself to the owner, Ellis McCrae. This will give you a feel for the lay of the land and win you some friends that could influence the way forward.'

Yeah, days are rolling away. I will get on top of things as soon as I have the details. Hoping to see you face-to-face, but that's up to Madame Tempest.'

'Be gentle with her. We need her. Rest first after that long flight.'

VIOLA POTTED AROUND THE APARTMENT, distracted by her two calls. The desire to hurry over to Porto lingered. Rob would seek her out whenever trouble brewed. Now she appreciated the need for a trusted ally as a leader. He had become restless with the antiquated thinking of the decision makers in town.

Tempest gave her room to get on with her job, but she felt a gnawing emptiness. Sebastian's arrival could help her forget she had the town's dead wood to contend with. Not much longer, she hoped.

Nothing in her life was complete. The need to feel grounded consumed her. If she had a child before it was too late, would she feel more settled in her life? But was having a child the answer, and with whom? She recalled blaming herself for her parents' break-up and Lorenza scolding her for such thoughts, telling her that a child does not ask to be born, and parents should consider carefully before they have a child.

Viola rose extra early to finish her paperwork. All night, her mind darted from Porto to Sebastian, and her unfulfilled longing for something she could not quite define.

13

The day brought unexpected news.

Sebastian slipped into town. A media *person* snuck in from the city a day before him sending Blackwater Ridge to the brink of a breakdown. Nobody knew who the media representative was. Mayor Corey's paranoia got the better of him if someone's credentials were elusive, even those who had been around him for decades. He stuck to his intimate associates, creating the perception that he was not a people person. Retirement beckoned, but he dug his heels in, a sculpted, cracking *Ozymandias* in a beautiful landscape.

Sebastian played the tourist, seeking quiet days.

Viola's early morning call from the police commissioner crushed her.

A senior student from Blackwater Ridge Performing Arts Academy disappeared overnight. Tamarind Jenkins was a Fine Arts major and music student. That was all Viola knew of her. Upon closer scrutiny in the school student files, she unearthed that Tamarind was a boarding student from Western Australia. Her parents were wealthy mining folk with ties to the shut mine at Blackwater Ridge. Tamarind boarded with her father's distant relatives, an elderly couple with no children of their own. Rob was not recovering as expected, which meant she had no sounding board on this recent development at the Academy. Her acting position's reins tightened with this news. Society's gaze, now a critical eye, would be cast in her direction, waiting for how she would react and support the Academy's community. The police commissioner could not confirm if the latest disappearance had any links to the other three.

Viola had to see Sebastian to set up his investigation plan. She would get involved, regardless whether Tempest opposed her decision. Tamarind disappeared under her watch. In desperate need of coffee, and the latest town news, she dashed over to Dukes for a word with Ellis. He would know more than the commissioner had told her.

Keeping everything calm at the Academy sat on her shoulders. Normalcy was paramount to keep students in their classrooms, undistracted by the news of Tamarind's disappearance.

It was a wet morning, and in her haste to see Ellis, she rushed out minus her umbrella. Ellis was in the doorway at Dukes, staring across the square. A light fog floated in from the beach, stealing the radiance of summer morning light. He turned when he heard hurried ticking heels. Viola's drenched, disheveled state made him squint before he realized it was her, under her dripping curls.

'Morning, Ellis. Another victim taken, the police commissioner confirmed.'

Her mournful look replaced her usual cheerful disposition.

'Morning, Viola. I don't know what to think. How are you holding up with this negative spotlight on the Academy? Look at you, saturated to the bone! Come inside and dry off.'

'Thank you. I am worried about my student. I might ask her parents to step in to help. Blackwater Ridge has served them well; they owe it to their daughter and the community to come forward.'

'I'm not sure if they know yet.'

'What do you mean? The commissioner must have called them first.'

'It's left to be seen. Folk with more than they need, preoccupied with wanting more than they have, find problems irksome to their life plans, you know.'

'I hear you. But I am intent on rolling in their support. They have influence to call in whatever we need.'

Ellis raised his eyebrows and stepped towards his office, urging Viola, with his dancing eyeballs, to follow him.

'What's wrong Ellis? Please don't ...'

He raised his hand to halt her gabble.

'Please listen to this, then tell me your thoughts.'

Viola inhaled, bracing herself for what Ellis was about to reveal.

'As I was locking the bar last night, I had a strange encounter. An old woman, who appeared perhaps around eighty, approached me, asking if she could speak to me. I was careful, unsure if this was a set-up or perhaps a staged hold-up. Before the young women disappeared, I would never have entertained such a thought, you know.'

She nodded and let Ellis continue.

'I have never seen this woman before, but she knew me by name and said she was from the caravanning community that came through town. Like I said, I have never seen her before last night, so my suspicions jumped into top gear. The media presence has me on my guard too, believing this could be a set-up for information. But as soon as she said she might have news on the missing women, I let her in.'

Viola was bursting to know what the old woman had said, but Ellis' panache to turn everything into a long story had to be given room to develop.

'I don't know what to make of it now after one of your students has disappeared.'

'Please, Ellis, tell me what the woman said. I am dying to know.'

'Give me a minute, I'm getting to it, trying to process it all and questioning myself whether she was telling the truth.'

Viola closed her eyes, took another deep breath to still her impatience as Ellis deliberated on his revelation.

'Well, she said they employed a trapeze artist a few months ago to work with the caravanner's children to get them to exercise and stretch their physical capabilities. Too much book work, she said, was not good for them. According to her, the young trapeze artist has gone AWOL in their community, devastating the children with his departure.'

'Right, so how does this tie in what's happening in Blackwater Ridge? Or do we presume she thinks he took our young women with him?'

'Yes, that's what she said. The time adds up with his unexplained departure and the three girls leaving.'

'And what about my student, this morning?'

Ellis shook his head. This seemed a lead worth following, but how and where? Andy's scarf-find and Ellis' recount of what the old woman told him were the only two pieces of nebulous information they had.

'You must pass this on to the police commissioner. Is the old woman still in town? Perhaps the commissioner and Mayor Corey could speak to her.'

Ellis shook his head, again much to Viola's annoyance.

'Why not? We cannot sit on the leads that come to us.'

'She begged me not to pass it on, but to investigate on my own. How am I supposed to do that, and run this business?'

Viola shot Ellis a curious look, suddenly suspicious of him.

'You can't be serious, Ellis! This is reportable information for which they can charge you for withholding crucial information from the police.'

'What is Corey going to do? And the commissioner is his stool pigeon. Forget it. All this information has done is give me a massive headache. It's on my shoulders now to find the missing young women.' He rolled his hands through his sparse hair signaling his anxiety.

'Time is running out. I must get to the Academy to meet with my staff to tell them what's happened to our student if they have not already heard the news. I'll call you later.'

Ellis walked away with Archimedes' gait; his shoulders ready to drop to the ground.

Viola prank called Sebastian, and he called her back from another number. She briefed him on what Ellis revealed and urged him to go down to Dukes to talk to Ellis. He would probably say more to a stranger than he would to her.

Most of the Academy's staff had not heard that their student had joined the ranks of the three missing girls. Andy knew from Mayor Corey's early morning call. The mayor was adept at disseminating information to a chosen few to preserve the silence. Viola advised staff to allow students to voice their feelings, assess anxiety and report to the counselor.

There was nothing more she could do. Sebastian was onto the case. He was her only hope inside the closed mindset of Blackwater Ridge.

* * *

SEBASTIAN WENT over to Dukes for morning breakfast, hoping Ellis would shed some light on the situation at Blackwater Ridge. Ellis slipped into his back office, leaving Sebastian at the mercy of his barista, another newcomer in town. Another strange was more than he could handle this morning.

The friendly barista smiled and asked in his customary way,

'How can I help you? You're new around here. I've haven't seen you before.'

'Thank you. Coffee to start, please. I am brand new in these parts. Just flew in from New York yesterday afternoon.'

'Wow, to what do we owe the honor, Mr New York?'

'I'm on a working holiday, the name's Seb Smith.'

He used his foster mother's surname. It was a half-truth name, and that was all he could offer in the moment.

The barista called out to Ellis to come over to meet their American visitor.

Ellis emerged with a worried expression.

'Hello, welcome. Are you a reporter for CNN or something?'

Sebastian extended his arm. 'Seb Smith, why would you think I'm a reporter?'

'Lots of strangers have arrived in town in a short space of time. It has me curious.'

There was something about Sebastian that convinced Ellis to apologize for his unfriendly suspicion. He saw an honest face and reached for Sebastian's extended hand.

'Nice to meet you, sorry for my suspicion. I'm Ellis, bar, and grill owner. Would you like our signature breakfast this morning?'

'Hm… yes, what is it?'

Sebastian rubbed his hands together like a boy who had won the bun and treacle race.

'All locally produced, our finest beef sausages, freshly laid eggs, fried to perfection, a side of baked beans and our own in-house damper.'

'Just what I need for my jet-lag on a rainy morning. The coffee is great.'

'Consider it a welcome to Blackwater Ridge breakfast on the house.'

Ellis beamed so much he threatened to outshine the absent sun this morning.

'Thank you, but that won't be necessary. You have a business to run.'

'What's your business, Seb?' Ellis asked with curiosity tinged with suspicion.

'I'm a writer seeking solitude and freedom from the hustle and bustle of city life.' Sebastian left out his academic work to buy him further anonymity for a few days, at least.

'Crime writer?' Ellis asked with another bout of renewed suspicion.

'No, I document findings on natural habitats, and I write a bit of poetry.'

'A poet! That is interesting. You should visit Blackwater Ridge Performing Arts Academy. I'm sure Ms Bardo would love to have you as guest poet at one of her assemblies.'

'Ms Bardo?'

Innocence oozed.

'She's the acting principal at the Academy.'

'I heard at the motel that a student disappeared from there.'

'Yes, the news sometimes spreads like wildfire in a small town.'

The barista reacted to this piece of news.

'Has another young woman disappeared?'

Ellis nodded. His face grave.

'A young woman came in with a backpack this morning for a coffee. She was in a hurry and did not want to miss the seven o'clock bus. She dashed out and left her coffee on the counter. I expected her to return, but that was it.'

'You should check this with Ms Bardo when she stops by later today.'

Sebastian cut in.

'Why wait for later today, talk to the principal now. That might actually shorten the search and perhaps ensure the student's safety.'

Ellis agreed and called Viola's PA to let her know his barista would stop by to see Ms Bardo when she could fit him in.

Sebastian left payment for his breakfast on the front counter and waved a goodbye as he slipped out of Dukes. He booked a hired car and set out on the road to observe and record his findings.

Sebastian's first step in the investigation kicked in.

14

Viola was knee deep in the missing young women's case. Sebastian's text message confirmed he was on the road for the next forty-eight hours on the heels of the caravanners.

She planned to meet him somewhere along the way – it was out of town, so no compromise to her position from prying eyes. Transport was a problem with her car sitting cobwebbed in her apartment garage. She never got rid of the car that caused her many haunted years. After her daring stint in Athens, in a life or death situation, she mustered the courage for a hellish drive away from the burning abandoned cottage. The accident ten years ago in Sydney froze her capacity to drive – a threat to her safety triggered a knee-jerk ride behind the wheel in Athens. She had to get her nerve back. There was no way she could hire a taxi to get to Sebastian. The curiosity of the driver would blow her cover.

Her stationery Subaru needed a thorough clean, and fuel, with at least one practice run around Blackwater Ridge before she could even think of going after Sebastian. Her crammed day with back-to-back meetings left no time to see Ellis' barista. She met him after her work day, he graciously agreed to wait around to see her after his shift.

After a long day locked in her office, the summer afternoon sun hurt her eyes on her walk to Dukes. A class photograph was all she had of the Academy's missing student, Tamarind Jenkins. She enlarged the image of the girl's face. If the barista confirmed the student's identity, then Sebastian was on a promising trail if the old woman told Ellis the truth.

Ellis' barista, Jake, sat in the far corner of the pub and waved to draw Viola's attention as she walked in. Ellis was out that afternoon and a new fresh-faced young man stood behind the counter. She greeted him and headed over to Jake.

'Thank you for agreeing to meet me after your shift. I see Ellis is not in. Does he have a new manager?'

'I want to help if I can. That's Jonas McCrae, Ellis' nephew, from Melbourne. He comes over to help whenever Ellis needs an extra set of hands.'

'When did he arrive?'

'Two days ago.'

Viola did a mental time check, everybody was a suspect in her book, until cleared.

'I see. Well, it's good that he has family here.'

'Yeah. Do you have a photograph I could look at? Sorry to rush you, but I am picking up the groceries tonight for a friend.'

'Yes, here it is.'

Jake studied the photograph and frowned.

'I'm not sure, but the person who hurried in for coffee had blonde hair. This student has dark hair.'

'What about her face, is it one you recall seeing?'

'I can't be sure, the image is pixelated.'

'Here, look again through my magnifying glass at the smaller image in the class group photograph. The enlarged copy might have distorted her features.'

Jake peered through Viola's magnifying glass and gasped.

'I think it's the same person. She must have been wearing a wig if her hair was blonde the morning I saw her.'

'Or dyed it. Are you a hundred percent sure she's the person who came in rattled for a cup of coffee?'

'I am ninety percent sure, now. It's the hair that adds a little doubt.'

'Thank you, that's all I needed to know.'

Jake, the out of towner barista was a good sort. He did not have to get involved but reported what he saw. She surveyed his body language. Could he be a suspect?

She stopped, startled, when Jake asked, 'Doing a bit of your own sleuthing, Ms Bardo?'

'What? No, not at all! I need the information for my records. I have to document everything that goes on during my acting post at the Academy.'

'If that's all you need, may I please leave to grab those groceries.'

'Certainly. Thank you very much for your time, Jake. May I buy you dinner soon?'

'That's kind of you! Thank you.'

He hurried off without an answer to her dinner invitation. And Viola knew that hanging around an acting school principal was not the cool thing for a young man to do.

Through their coding she let Sebastian know her student was somewhere with the other three missing students.

At Dukes. Coffee mate confirmed.

* * *

VIOLA DWELLED OVER ELLIS' recount of his conversation with the old woman who said she was from the caravanning community. Their recently appointed trapeze artist left without a word.

She looked up Tamarind Jenkins' profile on the Academy's portal. Tamarind was the Academy's top state gymnast, nominated to take part in the state championships in September. Could the trapeze artist have lured her away? Tamarind was a mature sixteen-year-old, boarding and managing her own life without her parents. All pistons fired in Viola's head, in her need to know everything about the trapeze artist. She had to speak to the woman to be a conduit to Sebastian on his hunt for the caravan community. Ellis had to cooperate with her on this, and Tempest needed an update on Sebastian's road trip.

Her last message to him was unanswered.

With Sebastian's intermittent communication, Viola had email contact only with Tempest.

The watch and wait began again.

She longed to have Rob's opinion of Tamarind Jenkins. Now she had to do what was in her student's best interest, with fragments of understanding on the girl's personality. She tossed aside her leadership hat to deal with tough decisions, just as Rob did.

Physical activity was the only way to still her anxious wait for a reply from Tempest. She went down to her basement garage to inspect her Subaru.

Thick dusty layers covered her car. The deep blue body indiscernible under woven cobwebs and a mat of dirt. She grabbed a mask, gloves, and her goggles out of the toolbox from the cupboard to the left of the car and busied herself with cleaning off years of unforgotten memories. Suddenly she heard the internal door to the basement shut, and jumped up to see who it was, but the person had gone. Had someone been watching her? Sebastian would laugh off such a thought, telling her she had an overactive imagination and should write novels instead of poetry. She missed his support and needed to articulate her thoughts with him. Nobody had her trust on the situation at the Academy. Right now, a process of elimination was necessary.

It was almost midnight when she got back to her apartment, covered in grime, and in need of a shower. Writing was the only way to process her thoughts. But it needed precision. She processed her thoughts in longhand.

I have not been this lonely in a long time. My childhood was an isolated one, with many hours on my own. I grew up with this expectation that I had to do everything alone, to achieve anything. Now, in this position I am there again, isolated in the privilege of having too much information available to me, but my guard is up on who I share it with. Darn! Am I turning into Mayor Corey?

If there is no news from Tempest by morning, I will have to ask Andy to step in and help me get my car started. My concern is if Sebastian is under threat in this situation, how will I support him? Andy might not be curious about my need to drive again – he knows nothing of my past. If Matthew were here, I would never second guess his trust. He's gone now. I pushed him out. He's hurt, I sense it. Lorenza no longer hears my cries. This leadership stuff is tough because I am the shoulder to all. My time at Aurora College was a walk in the park, but the days at the adult college in Porto were tricky. Vanessa Smythe was a strange leader. Heartless, really. A leader must be compassionate. Not free-and-easy but never Draconian. Perfection is impossible but balance is the magic needed for success. I am sure of that.

HER EYES GREW heavy and the words on the page hazy. More thoughts wafted in and out. Matthew deserved more. Fear left her isolated when commitment beckoned. She fell into an exhausted sleep and woke to the distant sound of her cell phone ringing. Her mouth was dry, and her body ached. She walked over to her impatient phone – too late, the caller left a message.

Ingrid Dwyer's message read:

Rob left this life in the early hours ...

15

Viola stared at Ingrid's message, paralyzed with fear. What would she do without Rob? Who would assume his position now? Rob had the answers to everything on running the Academy. Her to-go-to trusted person was no longer available. His tired body took an earlier exit than anticipated. Snatched! Nothing was certain. Everywhere she turned the stars misaligned in her orb. She dressed in zombie mode, and floated in a dark, heavy cloud down to Dukes.

Ellis was not in this morning.

Jake told her he had gone over to Rob's place to assist Ingrid with his funeral arrangements. Rob wanted a swift send off. Viola was aghast that she did not know this, but here was a stranger to Rob conveying intimate details on what he wanted for his final farewell.

The private side of life evaporates in death when one is no longer there to censor lips. This scared her. She had to have the last say on how people perceived her life. It was not up to strangers!

She grabbed her coffee to steel herself for a staff meeting this morning. She heard Ellis call out to her from the top of Illyria Square. He hurried towards her, his pink cheeks pale, his eyes dewy.

'Morning. Forgive me for calling out to you. I wanted to grab you before you set off for the Academy. Poor Ingrid, she's having a terrible time.'

'This is a shock to her, Ellis. She just lost her husband of many years.'

'I know, but she wants a very private funeral with three people present. You, me, and her, that's it.'

'Jake said something, that this was Rob's wish. Be careful what you say to him.'

'He must have overheard me talking to Ingrid. I said nothing to him except that I was going out for a short while.'

'You might have to caution him. Rob was a private man. I'm wondering now if I should I tell the Academy staff this morning, that there will be a private funeral to honor Rob. They would want a grand farewell. As much as Rob had a few staff members who opposed him, he was well-loved.'

'To be honest, I don't know what's the right thing to tell your staff. It was a tough conversation with Ingrid this morning, and I'm afraid I was not much help to her.'

'Don't be hard on yourself, Ellis. You are also grieving for a dear friend. I won't talk about the funeral then, just about how we plan to farewell Rob at the Academy.'

'That is probably the sensible thing to do, but the board would have their own plans too.'

'I don't know what happens with me in an acting capacity. The board has had no communication with me in the role.'

'Ingrid will advise you on that. She would talk to the board about Rob's last wishes, I suppose. Ingrid was his anchor, in her own quiet way, at home, and at work.'

'Yes, she was everything to Rob. I do not know how the

board can help. They have not come forward since our student disappeared.'

'Would you like me to speak to them about that?'

'No, please don't. I'll figure it out soon.'

They parted with heavy hearts. Their mutual friend, a man of deep conviction, one of the few in the town who called Mayor Corey on his errors of judgement and misguided decisions, yet never maligning him. Rob's professional repertoire kept him leading the Academy. Corey knew Rob's worth and had to pocket his pride by not pressuring the board to get rid of him.

At the staff meeting, a committee formed to prepare for the Academy's last farewell for Rob Dwyer. The staff respected Ingrid's need for privacy.

Viola shut her office door, put her head down on Rob's desk, and sobbed. Leaders had to hide a public show of emotions, that's how Rob ran his operation. While some thought him aloof and judged him on that assumption, he kept his emotions private to spare accusations of being weak. Rob took on the role of father, advising her decisions over their years together. Ingrid extended this by inviting Viola to Rob's birthday parties, for Sunday lunch, or an Easter feast, if she was in town.

Her PA canceled all external meetings for the day as a mark of mourning for Rob. She intended going over at midday to offer her condolences to Ingrid. She reached for her phone when an email notification popped up on her screen. She opened the email from Tempest, which left her numb.

Apologies, Viola, for my late reply. I am a tad unwell and will be in touch soon. My contacts are following up on the missing young women. - TT

THE HOLLOWNESS in her belly deepened. This was the first time the invincible Tempest had ever said she was unwell. Things were falling apart, and Viola had to keep herself intact. Thoughts jumped from one thing to the next. Ingrid replied it was ok to call at the house. The better part of the morning evaporated, with Viola staring out the window at the oval. At fifteen minutes to midday, she took a slow walk to Rob Dwyer's place, stopping off for a bunch of white roses at Maria's floristry. Rob loved roses, colorful roses, but all the color in the world departed with him today.

Ingrid looked thinner than when Viola last saw her two weeks ago. She had no visitors at the house during Rob's second recovery period. Ingrid hugged Viola at the door. She was alone, with no family to comfort her.

'Thank you for coming over, Viola. It means a lot to me. I know you feel Rob's loss as deeply as I do. You have been a daughter to him from the day you arrived in town. He has written you a letter which he instructed me to give you only after he took his last breath.'

Viola saw the tears in her eyes as she handed over Rob's letter.

'I am so sorry... sorry that you have to wind things up for Rob at the Academy. It is not the way he planned…'

Viola put the letter in her handbag. Her heart was heavy, but cautious not to upset Ingrid if she sobbed. Instead, she offered to make a cup of tea and spent two hours in long spells of silence with Ingrid staring at the wall in front of her, and then sharing fleeting recollections of her years with Rob.

Viola prepared a light dinner for Ingrid before she left. Her feet ached from standing in high heels for too long, and her head and heart separated with emotional exhaustion. Rob's letter peeped out the top of her bag. She ripped open the envelope.

My dearest Viola

I have gone by the time you read this. I told Ingrid to hold back, giving you my letter, until I had departed. You worry too much, and I hoped this would lessen your concerns. The Academy board, heaven help us, might not be ready to put a successor in place for some time. They are happy to have you filling in for me, but I emphasized that you would act only for the duration I discussed with you. I have wished you would take on the role in a permanent capacity but know you have plans and cannot stay indefinitely. So, all said, I appeal to you to pressurize the board for a replacement as soon as possible. When the position is advertised, please encourage Andy to apply. Second to you, Andy is the one who will carry forward the Academy with heart, soul, and diligence.

I sincerely apologize for the predicament I have put you in, with my untimely passing. I have known my number was being called just a week ago. The ticker has not been behaving for some time.

You will always remain in my heart as a teacher, with softness and strength. You are the daughter of my soul. Please watch over Ingrid for me whenever you can.

Your friend, always.

Rob Dwyer

PS. I fought the temptation to add 'Mr' to the front of my name because of your insistence on formality.

VIOLA HEARD his chuckle in his last words, her eyes fogged over, wetting the precious letter she clutched to her chest. She wished Sebastian were with her now, beside her, helping her through this. Grief was difficult to bear alone. She washed her face. Sobbed afresh, looked at her face in the mirror and said,

*Oh Rob, the only grief I've felt with such intensity before was
for Lorenza, now you. I promise to leave things as you would
have.*

She gave vent to her towering emotions in poetry.

> *the good all too soon gone*
> *floating away before day's done*
> *sailing to an unknown place*
> *while mere mortals push on*
>
> *promises made must be kept*
> *sealed in a bond before you left*
>
> *now I forge ahead to find a way*
> *with your name inscribed upon my lips*
> *ready to fulfil the task you ask of me*
>
> *only the best for the best*
> *never anything less*
>
> *forever and always may you rest*
> *cradled in peace*
> *resting in eternal sleep*
> *until we meet again*

VIOLA SAT with her open journal on her lap, pondering whether
Rob's fate could have been averted if he agreed to the surgery
earlier. He put the Academy first...

Nothing was going to raise Rob now – she had to accept that
cold reality.

She stood under the shower for an hour, thinking, sobbing,

hoping to have more news from Tempest with the promise of a call.

That night, her inbox was vacant.

Tempest had fallen into oblivion, and Sebastian was unreachable.

16

Twenty-four hours passed with no news from Sebastian. How would the investigation proceed without him, and Tempest's advice?

ON THE OUTSKIRTS OF TOWN, Sebastian caught up with the caravan community. It was 9 pm when he drove up to the laager nestled among pine trees, surrounded by a vast sun-bleached field swishing under a bright moon. The location was almost four hours out of Blackwater Ridge. The roving community headman, a lean tall man with a map-lined face, could have been in his mid seventies. When he spotted Sebastian's vehicle behind the caravans, he invited him in for tea.

'What are you doing in these parts at this late hour, lad?'

'I'm staying up in Blackwater Ridge and took a drive out to see more of what lay outside the town. I know it is a crazy thing to do as a stranger to the area, but I wanted to see more than just the town. My GPS signal died on me and I ended up here.'

'Technology is an unpredictable wife – can't live with her or without her!' He belched out an old smoker's raspy laugh, and Sebastian smiled. He disliked gendered language but had to let this one pass. The old man knew no better and meant no harm with his larrikin attitude. He said he had an old UBD, a bit out of date on the recent changes in Blackwater Ridge, but that Sebastian was welcome to make it his own.

'Thank you. That is very generous of you. I will sleep in the car until first light if that is ok with you?'

'We can't have that now! You are a stranger in these parts, you cannot escape your American accent, just as I can't hide my Aussie accent. It would be inhospitable to leave you to sleep in your car. It gets mighty chilly here past midnight. Come over to the camp, you can sleep the night in my trailer if you are prepared to take the top bunk.'

Sebastian grabbed the lucky moment.

'I don't want to inconvenience you or the community with my sudden arrival.'

'No inconvenience, we stopped over for two days, and I have a bed for you after one of our new recruits went AWOL recently.'

Into the lion's den! That was all Sebastian needed to quiz, this talkative, pixie-eyed, leather-faced man, into telling him more of what he needed to know.

The old man took Sebastian over to his trailer and stepped out to get him some food. He returned with an old woman. She held a plastic tray with a plate of chicken and potatoes and a cup of coffee she handed to Sebastian.

'Thank you so much. I am sorry to be troubling you this late in the evening.'

She ignored him and turned to face the old man.

'You picked up another one of these fellas? He'll disappear soon, just you wait and see.'

'He's passing through, that's all, he's American, visiting up in town. Let us show him our Aussie hospitality.'

She frowned at Sebastian and walked away, mumbling something incomprehensible.

'Old Bertha, she has a sixth sense for things, you know. She warned us about the trapeze artist who joined us to help the kiddies keen on learning such skills.'

'Any reason for his sudden departure?'

'Old Bertha seems to think he's involved with the missing women from Blackwater Ridge. She won't quite say what she knows.'

'Would she withhold important information if she does indeed know something?'

'You never know with that one, she can be odd, but the kiddies love her.'

'Don't we all have a bit of oddness? I would like to talk to her.'

'You should try in the morning, but I don't guarantee you will get anything from her.'

Fortune was on Sebastian's side.

'What's your name, lad? I'm Joshua but folks here call me Josh. I prefer Josh.'

'I'm Seb. Thank you for your hospitality tonight.'

'Well, Seb, you better chow down old Bertha's food or she will be mad as hell with you.'

'I will. I'm ravenous after that car trip.'

'Good night, I'm hitting the sack now. Be warned, I snore like a spluttering fleet of rusty trucks on a train track.'

Sebastian stepped out the trailer for some air when he noticed old Bertha sitting outside a caravan puffing a cigarette, three down from where he stood. This was a good time to engage her in conversation on what she knew about the Blackwater Ridge missing girls.

He walked over to her. She surveyed him with her head cocked to the right, her eyes slanted slits.

'What do you want? I don't like strangers wandering into my private time and space.'

'I beg your pardon, ma'am. I could not sleep and am keen to know more about this place.'

'So, you think the old woman can help you? I have been traveling in this community since the age of nine. I've seen many arrive, leave or stay on as family and die here too.'

'May I chat with you for a wee while?'

'So, what do you want to know, young man?'

'I would love to hear your life story.'

'How long are you staying? There's mighty much to tell.'

'I'm leaving as soon as I know my way back. Start wherever you like. I'm eager to know about the folk here, and I'm a good listener.'

Sebastian saw a fleeting smile and a brief light behind her eyes.

'I need to know who I'm talking to, what's your name? What are you, a journalist or police?'

'Seb, ma'am. Neither. Just a traveler. How should I address you?'

'Bee will do. I hate being called Bertha. Josh probably told you I was 'Old' Bertha. He forgets he's Old Josh.'

Bee laughed and coughed. Smoking was the pastime in this community, where time was not a priority.

She spoke of the years when care, loyalty and trust were important to the community. The younger ones grew restless, and some moved on while others looked for new ways to entertain themselves. Bee had no children of her own. All the children in the community looked up to her as a mother figure.

'I have babysat many of the young ones when their parents picked up casual work as we passed through different towns. Parents were generous back in the day, buying me food or clothes. Money is not the currency here, Seb, we share all we have, well the older ones still do.'

'That must be an amazing way to live. Materialism has smothered the modern world.'

'That's the sad state of our lives today. That is why we have crime, such as the young women disappearing with no warning.'

Sebastian's heart thumped! The door was wide open to tap into what Joshua told him about the trapeze artist. He chose not to mention Ellis or Viola having this information.

'Josh mentioned the trapeze artist suspicion you have regarding Blackwater Ridge's missing young women.'

'That Josh has a mouth on him! He refuses to believe me but sees fit to tell you.'

'I'm happy to hear what your speculations are on this matter.'

'Speculations? Saw it with my own two eyes. Everything else might have aged, but not my eyes. I can see as clear as day as I did at nine years old.'

'I wish I had perfect vision. I wear reading glasses.'

'That's because your phone and computer are your everything, arms, legs, body. You ruined your eyes.'

'This is true.' Sebastian's acceptance seemed to ease Bee's caution.

'That trapeze artist had too smooth a tongue for my liking. I cautioned Josh about not taking him in. But Josh has this big old soft heart like us rustic folk do. A woman knows what she knows, so I warned him. Old Bertha knows things, Seb, just you hear me out.'

Bee said that when they got news from Blackwater Ridge that the young women had left in the early hours of the morning and nobody had a clue where they were, she told Josh about her suspicion when the newcomer trapeze artist did not return to their campsite that day.

Sebastian did not interrupt the one who *knew things*, but he was bursting to find out how the caravanners got wind of the news from town.

'When Josh would not listen to me, I hitched a ride on the bus passing through to town and went to Dukes to see the owner, Ellis McCrae. He is like the town crier or whatever you call them folk who have their ears to the ground. He told me to go to the police. No way was I doing that, so I left. I am only the messenger.'

Sebastian studied Bee's face and knew she was telling the truth. He had to let her tell her yarn before he asked questions.

She said because she suspected the newcomer had sinister intentions; she snooped around.

'He seemed to strike up a close friendship with Harold, Joshua's son, and that fella is a worthless, lazy piece of flesh, if ever I saw one. Well, here's the thing. One night I stood in the shadows close to Harold's caravan. I heard two male voices and knew the trapeze artist was in there with him. It horrified me when I heard girls' voices among them! What those scoundrels were doing with girls in the caravan, is something I don't want to know.'

Sebastian sighed, terrified that this was leading to what Viola dreaded.

'Then a car with its headlights turned off, pulls up and a woman with long dark hair comes out and it looked like three teenage girls, left with her. The next day there was no sign of the young trapeze artist – gone!'

Sebastian broke in at this point in Bee's recount.

'My goodness! That's it! Did you speak to Joshua about what you saw?'

'I told him, but he brushed it aside like I was mad.'

'What about Ellis, did you tell him all of this?'

'No, I did not tell him about Harold. I don't want to get involved with the police. Josh knows and now you.'

'You know I cannot withhold evidence now that I know.'

'Do what you have to, but don't involve me. I want peace, please, but I want the girls found and returned home.'

'Thank you for sharing this, Bee. I think this will bring them home if nothing awful has happened to them. I fear for their lives.'

'Nobody's gone and killed them! No, the trapeze artist was not a violent man, just too eager to please with that smooth talk. I don't think he harmed the girls. Harold will know where they are.'

Sebastian had all he needed to hear. He left when Bee retired for the night and snuck back to Blackwater Ridge, while Joshua snored to his heart's content.

17

Sebastian arrived at Blackwater Ridge as the night staff changed over shift at the bedsitter. For a small town, the bedsitter ran like a fully operational hotel. The manager noticed his unshaven face.

'Everything ok, sir? Can I get you anything?'

'All good, thank you for asking. I lost my way on the drive out yesterday when my phone died on me, and I had no bread-crumbs to find my way home.'

He laughed, expecting the manger to join in but had no reaction.

Sebastian put it down to being dumbstruck that their American guest was wandering overnight on the outskirts of the town.

His message to Viola and her immediate response told him she was on tenterhooks, worrying about his whereabouts.

'Meet me at the beach in half an hour in your walking gear, and I'll explain it all.'

Viola decided it was time to break Tempest's rule on not meeting Sebastian face-to-face. With no contact from Tempest, they had to steer the operation. Viola arrived at the beach ten minutes before Sebastian and overlooked his tardiness when he arrived with two large *Campos* coffees.

'Thank you, Sebastian. Boy! Am I glad to see you! Not having word from you, stressed me, and I fear Tempest might be ill. Her silence is worrying.'

'I am also concerned that Tempest is unreachable. Let me tell you what I've discovered during my night-time wanderings.'

Viola did not expect to hear that Tempest had abandoned the airwaves with Sebastian. She was never unresponsive or late without a forewarning. A promise from her was made in blood.

'I am worried that her absence, for one, is uncharacteristic, and that her cough was frequent when we last spoke. Her voice was raspier.'

'I'm sure she will be in touch soon. Listen to this. Shall we walk further down the beach to avoid anyone overhearing us, especially the journo from the city?'

Sebastian told her everything he had heard from Bee.

'That information reveals nothing about my missing student. Is she tied to the same case is what I need to find out?'

'I think she is. The trapeze artist must have her at another location. I have to pass this info to the police commissioner without creating the impression that I am unofficially investigating the case.'

'There's someone heading towards us from the road. I'll turn around and head home and you go to the police station. I forgot to mention that my car is available for you whenever you need it, anytime. Come over to the apartment when you can, and I'll give you a set of keys.'

'That will link us. Not a good idea! Tempest did not want that.'

'Right now, I do not care about that. Gotta go as do you!'

'Aye, captain, I will do that now. I'll come over to your place tonight.'

Viola plugged in her headphones and ran past the advancing stranger.

Sebastian watched her speed off, kicking up sand as she headed for the road. It amazed him that she flouted Tempest's rule of no face-to-face contact on this mission. She diligently heeded Tempest's instructions to the letter. Sebastian heard a voice call out to him to stop. He ignored the call and walked on.

'Excuse me. Wait up a minute, please.'

A middle-aged man, with graying temples, in a pair of faded blue jeans caught up with him and stood in front of him, forcing him to stop.

'Was that Ms Bardo from the Academy that I saw running up to the road? I have to talk to her.'

'Who are you, and why do you need to talk to Ms Bardo?' Sebastian stepped back to survey the intrusive man.

'Jim Halloran, North Star News. I am here to report on the missing student from the Academy.' He extended his hand. Sebastian ignored his gesture.

'In that case you should make an appointment with Ms Bardo rather than hope to accost her during her run on the beach.'

'I saw you both chatting and figured you have a hand in the case?'

Sebastian walked away, leaving a gob-smacked Jim Halloran staring after him.

* * *

SEBASTIAN HEADED to the police department to report what he heard from Bee.

He received a hostile attitude which he did not expect after the hospitality he received at the bedsitter, and from Josh and Bee. The commissioner cross-questioned him as though he were the guilty party.

'Who did you say you are?'

'I didn't, actually. I'm on a sabbatical, I am a New Yorker. Seb, Seb Smith.'

'Why did you choose our backwater town for your sabbatical?'

'I needed the peace and slow pace.'

The commissioner cast him a dubious look.

'So, you heard all this information from an old woman?'

'A wise and upstanding old woman named Bee whose wit is sharper than most people I've met.'

Sebastian left that open to avoid riling the commissioner and risking him shutting off.

'I will pass this information on to our mayor and let him decide on the next course of action.'

The spineless commissioner, much to Sebastian's surprise, could not make a decision on an investigation he should be heading.

'May I assist with some of the investigative work?'

'Thank you, we've got this. I'll let you get on with your peace and slow pace in our town.'

Sebastian felt his bite in those words and understood Viola's perception of the leaders in Blackwater Ridge. Strangers would never be privy to the inside story of the town.

He went over to Dukes to offload his irritation.

Ellis was alone at the bar after the early morning rush.

'Good morning Ellis.'

'Hey, the Americano returns! I wondered what happened to you. I figured the eggs might have been over easy and the bacon too dry for your New Yorker standards!' His guffaw had Sebastian laughing. Ellis reached over to lock knuckles with him.

'I am here for that scrumptious Dukes' special breakfast and will be in your face every morning from here on, well while I'm in Blackwater Ridge, that is.'

'Good to know, mate. So, what have you been up to?'

'If you can spare me a moment to lend me your ears, I need to speak with you in private. Can we talk in your office?'

Ellis narrowed his eyes, wondering what this newcomer he had come to like had to share.

'Sure, step into my office, it's quiet and locals holler if I'm not at the counter when they come in.'

Sebastian told Ellis all that had happened on his night jaunt to the caravan community and the police commissioner's response to his offer of help.

'I can't say I'm surprised he shut you down. That's the way things are around here. You must earn your colors. That code of secrecy ethic. Mayor Corey will never allow a new bloke in town to steer his ship, least of all, a passing stranger. No offence to you, but this is how this place rolls. It's a great pity that good folk aren't trusted enough when they can make a difference.'

'Like yourself Ellis.'

Ellis shook his head. 'There is no way that I will ever want to allow myself to be coerced into taking on a leadership position. Dukes, is all I need, and enjoy. But I wish Corey would loosen up and let go of the reins sometime soon. This town is crying for change.'

'Do you think they will take action on what I reported today?'

Ellis tapped his fingers on his desk and ran his fingers through his hair.

'Hard to say, you know. Too much time has passed since the first young woman left. Andy from the Academy is the one to talk to. He would be keen to know what you have to say. Truth is, I think he would be an ideal leader for Blackwater Ridge. If you come back around 5 pm, you could chat with him then. He pops over like clockwork every day after work.'

'Yes, sure, thanks Ellis. I would rather pass this on to someone who will do something with the information.'

Ellis smiled. 'Who knows, Corey might like you as one who is not here to revolutionize his town.'

'Let's wait and see what Andy suggests. Catch you later, Ellis.'

Sebastian knew why Viola was fond of Ellis. His open and friendly nature survived the clandestine leadership of the town. There was much to report to Tempest, but each time he rang her, his call went unanswered. This had never happened before. Without email and telephone contact with her, decisions had to be made quickly. Neither he nor Viola knew where she lived or the location of her vigilante agency. After his meeting with Andy, he had to persist with getting hold of Tempest.

* * *

ON VIOLA'S END, the Academy board chairperson, Lawrence Hargreaves, contacted her, asking her to remain as acting head until they found a suitable replacement for Rob. He told her they wanted no interruptions to the academic year by further movement in the role, which carried the risk of losing students and staff. She asked for a few days to think through their offer.

'Take all the time you need,' Lawrence Hargreaves told her, adding to her sense of guilt if she vacated the post before they were ready. Rob left a warning to watch Hargreaves without saying much, apart from he had mellowed somewhat over the years, but needed to be watched.

1 8

A t 5:15 pm, Andy and Viola walked into Dukes. Sebastian sat at a corner table up against the wall at the back of the bar and grill, waiting for Ellis' introduction to Andy. Viola's presence posed a level of awkwardness for no one else but Sebastian. He was mindful never to flout Tempest's instructions – this was beyond his control.

Ellis walked up to him, with Viola and Andy in tow.

'Seb, this is Andy I spoke of, and you have the good fortune of meeting Ms Bardo, Viola Bardo, acting head at the Academy.'

Sebastian was quick to deflect Viola's wide-eyed, helpless *what should we do look.*

'I met Viola at the beach the other day, so we are somewhat acquainted.'

Ellis clapped his hands in delight.

'Well, what do you know, Blackwater Ridge is indeed a small town after all!'

His laughter rang across the room, enlivening Dukes with his much needed merriment.

'I take it then that you are comfortable with Viola sitting in on our gathering. She is the most trusted person around here.'

'I might get a big head now, Ellis. Your compliments are way too generous.' Viola looked over at Sebastian.

'Any friend of yours, Ellis, is most welcome.' Sebastian winked at Viola.

This fortuitous meeting with Viola was a relief in knowing he would not have to explain it to Tempest. The beach walk meeting was easy to explain because of the urgency of the situation.

Andy listened, leaning across the table not to miss a word from the softly spoken Sebastian.

'Thank you so much for sharing this with us. No doubt the police commissioner will sit on his laurels, waiting for Corey to give him the go-ahead. I'm going out tonight in search of this trapeze artist!'

Andy was fired up, and nothing was going to stop him.

Ellis gave Viola a worried look.

'Hang on, Andy. You must think this through first. We don't know what danger lurks on this.'

'Exactly, the young women are in danger and I am not wasting another minute waiting for someone else to do something, which is nothing! Viola, may I take some French leave please?'

Viola sighed and rolled her eyes, and Andy accepted that as her approval.

She had to choose her words wisely. Sitting in the privileged position of her beloved Rob was not something to toy around with. His name and his belief in her had to be upheld. Many long-standing residents, such as Andy, received no recognition for the role. Today, Andy's call to action would have received Rob Dwyer's unremitting support.

Andy left to organize his night search and Sebastian walked Viola home. She invited him in for a drink.

'I have to pass on the drink. I intend to join Andy on his search tonight. I need a clear head, as do you for your day tomorrow, Ms Bardo.'

'Are you sure about this, Sebastian? It could get messy when small town politics kicks in.'

Viola's older sister voice, much like Lorenza's tone with her, emerged when she felt concerned for the young and restless.

'A hundred percent! I must call Tempest. I could not reach her with my last five calls.'

Viola's frown line, above her nose, deepened to a permanent fixture.

'Yeah, I'm concerned about her unresponsiveness, it's not like her at all. You should let Andy know you are joining him on this hunt tonight. Don't just turn up and surprise him, he will not be happy with that.'

'I don't have his details. It might help if you called to say I should tag along.'

Viola confirmed Andy was happy to have Sebastian as co-partner. Fabian had to stay at the Academy. Two teachers out on the same mission would spell trouble with the staff.

Viola handed over her car keys to Sebastian and took him to her basement garage.

'Wow, your car is in mint condition. Why have you parked it off?'

'It has had an auto-valet overhaul in time for your use. And as for why it is a museum piece, I will explain once this is all over.'

Later that night Andy and Sebastian set out to find the trapeze artist Bee spoke of.

* * *

ROB'S BURIAL was arranged for 11 am the next day. Viola picked up her laptop to scroll through her emails that seemed to pile up by the minute. An unknown sender grabbed her attention.

Richard Monroe and Associates.

Half hesitant that it might be a spam email, she was about to delete it, but curiosity got the better of her. The first line sent a cold, rolling shiver through her.

Dear Ms Bardo

Richard Monroe and Associates are attorneys that represent our client, Tempest, as you know her. We regret to advise that she is gravely ill and has asked us to...

A lump hardened in Viola's throat, and an overwhelming rush of emotions quickened her heart. She sat back in her chair, her brow damp. No, not Tempest, this was too sudden! The email advised that Tempest was in surgery and that Viola would receive an update soon on when Tempest would be in touch. *Richard Monroe and Associates* advised that Viola could do whatever was needed to action a just and safe outcome for the missing young women.

This was Tempest's relinquishing of her direction. She was passing on the responsibility, and Viola did not know the nature of her illness or what her surgery entailed. Tempest – mysterious even when she was most vulnerable. Viola's vigilante role gave her a second life. Did this spell its demise? She fought back tears that blurred the words in front of her. Amid the confusion of her thoughts, she lost track of time until the room brightened with morning sunlight beaming through her half-drawn blinds. She needed some sleep before she faced another emotional morning at Rob's last rites. No beach walk, not today.

Viola curled into a ball and forced her eyes shut.

* * *

TWO HOURS later Ellis called as she got out the shower. He was waiting outside her apartment to walk with her to the chapel on the hill. Ingrid would meet them there.

Ellis saw Viola's wrecked state.

'Got little sleep, huh?'

'Yeah, I struggled through the night.'

Ellis put his arm around her shoulder. Something he had not done before.

'We are going to be there for Rob and Ingrid. I know you can do this.'

His kindness set her off in a wave of sobs. They paused on their walk to the chapel. Ellis held her hand, and she told him her concern that Sebastian headed out with Andy last night, and she was anxious about seeing Ingrid at the chapel.

'That's pretty decent of Seb to help Andy. I knew he was a good sort from the day we met. Now, let us do this for Rob.'

Without another word, they reached the chapel on the hill.

Father Angelo was in quiet conversation with Ingrid.

The chapel was cold. Viola shivered when wind gushed in and a kookaburra broke the silence in its noisy flight.

A small, still farewell for Rob Dwyer was as he lived his life.

No pomp — a humble send-off for a grand man.

Ingrid, stoic, as Rob would have expected, her hair and make-up perfectly in place, but her black sleeveless dress revealed her bony arms. She was withering away in the silence of her struggle, a face of bravado crumbling inside. Rob's letter asked for Viola to look in on Ingrid whenever she could. She made a promise to herself to live up to Rob's request.

At the crematorium, Viola crumbled in uncontrollable sobs. Here was the man who filled the shoes of her second father. Ellis and Ingrid hooked their arms through hers as they sent off the man they dearly loved. A grand man in a simple send off by only the people he wanted, and Ingrid honored his wish.

They headed for Duke's after settling Ingrid at the house. Ellis shut the place to the public for the day as a mark of mourning for Rob.

'I need a drink, as I'm sure you do. Let's sit awhile. Call your PA and cancel your afternoon.'

Ellis knew Viola needed company today to distract her.

Viola's heightened dread over Tempest's ill health compounded her sadness that Rob was no longer a telephone call away.

Ellis offered to walk her home. She declined and took a stroll to the beach. She needed the waves crashing on the shore to deafen her aching thoughts and shattered heart.

Two minutes down the beach walkway, she heard hastening footsteps behind her.

'Ms Bardo? Viola Bardo?' A male voice called out quite close behind her.

She stopped, turned on her heel.

'Who are you? How do you know me?'

'Phew! I'm so glad I caught you. I'm Jim Halloran, city journo. May I speak to you for a minute? '

Viola felt the chapel chilliness surround her again.

'You've had your minute.' She turned and quickened her step away from him.

'I'm not reporting on the missing young women, if that's what you think. I am here to do a feature on Rob Dwyer. He was a prominent name in educational circles.'

Viola thawed, stopped, and turned to a small face with pleading, kind eyes. Perhaps he was not the devil journo the town feared since his arrival.

'You would have to speak to Mrs Dwyer about that. It is not my place to offer information on her husband, or her family. We cremated him this morning. She needs to mourn her husband.'

She thanked him and walked away.

Then she heard him say, 'Will you ask her for me, Ms Bardo?'

'It's too soon.'

19

Andy and Sebastian visited all the motels along the periphery of Blackwater Ridge.

Ten kilometers outside the town center, a motel owner revealed what had disturbed him. Staff heard voices from the room a young man rented. The occupants placed the *Do not disturb* sign permanently on the door, barring cleaning staff from getting in for a room refresh. Meals were not ordered from the motel kitchen, but the young man left every morning and evening and returned with four brown paper bags each time. He paid his bill and left alone two days ago. The room the unseen guests occupied was tidy except for damp towels and used toiletries as the telltale signs of its occupants. No one saw them arrive or leave.

Sebastian asked the motel owner to describe the young man and what he got was that the man moved liked a ballet dancer. This confirmed he was the trapeze artist. If he left two days ago, he could be a long way off. Andy recommended they question the owners of the sparse stores in the area. If the young man returned with brown bags of food, he must have shopped in the area.

'He could have traveled to the next town if he did not want to be remembered.'

'Who would serve food in brown bags in these parts?' Sebastian asked.

Andy looked up an online map and discovered an eatery five kilometers west of the motel. The eatery, attached to a petrol and service station was their first checkpoint.

Andy pulled up outside the eatery around 7 am after sleeping overnight in the car, avoiding local accommodation to prevent drawing curiosity to their presence. The notice board outside the run-down servo proclaimed serving the freshest sandwiches, homemade pies, freshly baked each day, and bacon and egg rolls as the best in the Southern Hemisphere.

'Just what the belly is crying out for right now after a rough night!' Andy laughed.

Sebastian walked into the servo, and Andy topped up the petrol.

A tall, round woman appeared as soon as the bell tinkled above Sebastian's head, announcing his arrival.

'Good morning! I followed my nose from ten kilometers away! I sure need me some of them homemade meat pies and filtered coffee, ma'am.'

The woman was quick to respond.

'Well, you sure have come a long way from American shores.'

'Is my Aussie accent that bad?'

'It sounds like nothing I've ever heard around here, and I've been here for twenty-five years!' The woman's husky laugh and tobacco breath confirmed a chain smoker.

'Busted as charged. I'm here with my Australian mate. He is out there, filling up the tank.'

'I see. Good on you for trying, but even the kangaroos would know you're a foreigner. What's your name, young man, and what can I get you?'

'Seb Smith's the name, ma'am. Two flat whites please and a beef pie with a generous dollop of gravy will do me fine. My friend will decide what he's eating when he comes in.'

'Coming up! Excellent choice, the pies are just this minute out of the oven.'

'I told you I followed my nose!'

Sebastian kept it light and jolly. The woman was a talker, and that was just what they needed.

'What's your name ma'am, do you bake these beauties yourself?'

'Maud, it's Maud Cartwright. I sure bake them myself, 3 am every day, seven days a week, for the last two decades. My grandpop's recipe. He was a mean pie-maker. Folks would drive in from the city to get his pies.'

'Wow! That sure is commitment. Do a lot of folks pass through here?'

'Yeah, truckers and foreigners like yourself, Seb.'

'Looks like I should move here. I make a mean apple pie if I say so myself.'

'Good on you, lad! I like a good-looking fella who can cook and clean!'

Sebastian's nervous giggle and Andy's tinkling arrival were just at the right moment. Sebastian half expected Maud to slap a wet kiss smack on his lips.

'Hey Seb, good call to stop, it smells like heaven in here.'

'Now there's a familiar true-blue accent!'

'Andy, this is Maud, store owner and baker extraordinaire!'

'Only a home-grown lad appreciates home styled food. Seb's probably used to his American fast food. What would you like, Andy?'

'Beef pie, please.'

'Well, both you fellas have good taste. Your mamas raised you well. Take a seat out the back, I'll bring your pies to you.'

Sebastian wished he had such a mama, but laughed and nodded.

Once Maud was out of earshot, Sebastian whispered.

'She's a talker, and curious too, just what we need.'

Five minutes later, Maud shuffled out into the cool outdoor air with a tray of steaming beef pies.'

'Oh, I ordered one pie,' Sebastian exclaimed.

'One is on the house. Hungry lads need more than one pie each!'

'I won't argue with that.'

'How about joining us for a cupper?' Andy asked Maud.

'I'm sure you're just being kind. Who wants an old biddy hanging around?'

'Come on now, old biddy? Far from it! Please join us. Tell us about these parts.'

'All right, if you insist. Hang on, I'll get a coffee and be back. Mind you, I have tobacco breath which could knock your socks off. A bad habit I can't kick, I'm afraid.'

Maud retuned with a mug the size of a jug and a bacon and egg roll.

'You run the business on your own, Maud?'

'For the past five years, after my husband died. My niece comes and goes, so I'm not entirely on my own.'

'That's good that you have someone to help you.'

'I don't know that she's much help. She mentioned the other day that she was thinking of joining the trapeze bloke and his troupe to perform on his shows. You fellas looking for work?'

Sebastian shot Andy a winning lottery look.

'That sounds exciting. How did she meet him?'

'He popped around for a few days to get meals for his team and got chatting with my niece.'

'Gymnasts training out this way, that's intriguing.'

'He was quite a nice, polite young man. What a body on him!

Like Rudolph Nureyev, the Russian dancer, you know. Gosh, my old heart did a skip or two each time he came in dressed in a singlet, mind you. That would be a big reason why my niece wants to run after him!' She laughed and coughed.

'Has she gone off with him? Where is he now?'

'Who knows with these young ones? Said he was heading for Sydney. Some show there or something.'

Both Andy and Sebastian exclaimed, 'Sydney!'

'Why the surprise, fellas?'

'That's a long way off from here.' Andy said.

'Long way off from what?'

'My niece, or rather my wife's niece, has disappeared from Blackwater Ridge, so I'm wondering if she might have joined his troupe. If he headed to Sydney, it will be difficult to track him down in that overcrowded metropolis!'

'I'm truly sorry to hear about your wife's niece. That's really rough! Well, you both are a decent sort, it seems. If you stick around until this afternoon, my niece could tell you more. That's if you want to risk waiting, or I could call and ask her. You're not coppers, are you?'

'Nah! Just a pair of good guys who want to do the right thing. We'll wait around,' Andy said, 'if you have any odd jobs around the place, we could help.'

Sebastian remained mute. He was no handyperson. All he could do was pass around a hammer and nail!

'Sweet! I think I will take you up on that! Only if lunch is on me.' Maud's glistening face and broad smile revealed quite a few missing teeth.

'Done! Where shall we start?' Andy exclaimed in anticipation of lunch.

'A shelf needs to be put up in my storeroom and the outside toilet needs a seat fitted. I bought it months ago and never got around to fitting it.'

'Lead us to it, Maud,' Andy said with a reluctant Sebastian sauntering behind him.

What they expected to hear from Maud's niece was anyone's guess.

2 O

Tempest was out of surgery.

Her lawyer, as promised, kept Viola informed. She was in recovery, and the minute she was strong enough, she would be in touch with Viola.

Viola's reaction to the first sign of trouble around her was to reach out to those she could assist. Now she had no way of soothing Tempest, easing her load, or taking care of her emotional needs. Tempest was a silent force behind her. With the third-party legal intervention between them, she could not act in a personal capacity to repay the favors granted to her. Tempest's age and face were unknown to Viola. This need-to-know gnawed like it had never done before. Empathy was Viola's natural inclination. She regretted not probing for personal details from Tempest. She was a voice over the airwaves, that was all, and yet her mysterious presence was magnetic. Serving justice took priority. The trivial who and why of the every day had no significance or space in their lives. Tempest was just Tempest, an ethereal being never seen in the physical form. No history, no details but bearing the properties of a tempest in rushing in and out when situations demanded her guidance. Depressing thoughts engulfed Viola – was this Tempest's last outpost? This, jarring thought, invited guilt for not having called Placido for many days. Their father-daughter pact was only forty-eight hours of non-communication.

It was ten in the morning in Porto, Placido would be in his office. Viola called, and her father picked up almost instantly.

'Artista! Meu filho, I was worried not hearing from you, but like a good father I was going to give you until tonight, my time, before I called you. I know you are busy but one brief text message to your old papa is all I need to know you are doing ok.'

'Oh papa! I miss you. I am so sorry for not keeping to my promise. Too much going on at all levels here. But it's a paltry excuse. I'm sorry.'

'All's not lost. Make sure you are taking care of yourself. Eat well. Sleep for reasonable hours. These are important things for your wellbeing. Now can you tell me what you've been busy doing.'

'Work is busy, and Tempest is out of action.'

Placido jumped in before she could finish saying what she had to.

'Out of action? How is that possible? She is your leader, meu filho.'

'She is a fine leader and more, but she's had some surgery this weekend, and my only means of communication is through her lawyer.'

'I hope she recovers soon. Stay close, listen to everything her lawyer says.'

'Thank you, I will, papa.'

Viola took advice from her father with the ease of a docile child. She told him the bare bones, and he accepted and trusted that she knew what she was doing. Deep down he understood Tempest filled a mother yearning in his Artista. From what little he knew of Tempest, she was a good role-model for his daughter. With Lorenza's unsolved disappearance, their family had never recovered. As a doting father he wanted his Artista to be settled, to have someone to love and be loved.

'Have you heard from Matthew, recently?'

'Why papa? Has something happened?'

Viola jumped to attention. It was odd that in the middle of discussing Tempest; her father asked about Matthew Soto.

'No, no, no, meu filho! Nothing is wrong! That mind of yours is jumpy! You need some meditation time. I think you feel stressed over Tempest, right?'

'Yes, I am but... or forget it. No, I have not heard from Matthew. You might know what I don't know, so tell me, papa, how is Matthew?'

'Call him meu filho. You need a friend now with all this business going on. He's good for you. I saw that when he was in Porto over Christmas.'

'You mean *friend*, not anything more, dear papa?'

'A friend, meu filho, I'm not suggesting anything else, or you will snap up my head!'

Placido laughed, hoping to unwind his daughter's pent-up state.

'I will call him soon, I promise, that's if he's up to talking to me.'

She knew her father was looking out for her happiness after his own unhappy marriage. It left him depressed and lonely. Viola needed a better end of the stick in life. She had a rough childhood with their constant bickering. An only child imbibes every hurt of their storming parents.

'What do you mean by saying that?'

Viola's silence was a signal for Placido to stop probing. Helena's badgering scarred her, always wanting her daughter to do as she wanted.

'How's Ariel, papa?'

'I think she's ok? I don't see her, nor hear her. Such a sprite is she!'

'Papa! Seriously, how is she?'

'Busy, remarkably busy. We have been collaborating on a collection, so it's been head and shoulders to the wheel. Ariel is an old soul and enjoys solitude, so I try not to intrude. No laughter rings through the gallery like it does when you are here, Artista. But I am happy, she is here.'

Viola felt a tinge of sadness. Her father was a bright spark, as much as he was a dark soul. He lived these opposites, but when she was away, he vacillated more to sadness.

'It makes me feel better if you are happy.'

'I know you are busy, meu filho, and understand if you can't call every week, but a wee text message to tell me you are ok, but busy, is all I need. Will you do that?'

'Thank you, papa, I will send a message if I can't call you.'

Viola toyed with the thought of calling Matthew and gave up. She did not have the emotional capacity to endure his awkward silences, and the mammoth effort needed to stop him from feeling wounded from their departure in Porto. She needed time to get her head and heart around the intimacy that grew between them at the gallery. He felt spurned. She moved on, or so she thought.

A message to Sebastian instead did not bring the comfort she needed.

His words stared off the lit screen.

Nothing yet.

It was close to 9 pm when on an impulse she strolled down to Dukes. Ellis would be closing for the night. In recent days he shut the pub earlier than usual. Viola needed company, and Ellis was a good listener and the town's oracle.

He was wiping down the front counter.

She called out, 'Late night patron, may I come in?'

'Viola! This is a surprise, seeing you at this hour. But a pleasant one! Need a drink? I sure as hell do!'

'Sounds good, gin please.'

'Everything ok? You look exhausted.'

'I don't know Ellis. I hoped you might have news to share.'

'I have something to tell you, but I'm not sure how you will feel about it.'

'How about you tell me first and then I'll tell you how I feel.'

They both chuckled and sipped on their gin.

Ellis told her he spoke to Mayor Corey about Bee's speculations and told him Andy and Sebastian were out investigating where the trapeze guy was. Mayor Corey was furious and saw it as an interference with due process. He sent out the police commissioner to bring them back.

Viola sucked in her breath.

'Oh, Ellis, this might ruin Andy's chances of finding the young women. I believe he's onto the right lead.'

'Look, I am over the inertia in this town. This might shake up Corey and his commissioner into actioning a town search. Corey needs to feel threatened, you know, a bullet up the creek to do anything. Sorry, I am just over this town secrecy image rubbish!'

Viola had never witnessed this intensity in Ellis before, and knew it was overdue. Perhaps the commissioner heading out to find Andy and Sebastian might prove positive.

Ellis poured her another gin. He was nowhere near wanting to shut shop for the night.

'What made you stay on in this town? You are a forward-thinking man, so why stay?'

'I don't know, perhaps a misguided sense of wanting to give back for the childhood I had here. My family spans many generations in these parts, so it's some… allegiance, I suppose.'

'Nothing wrong with that. So, you never ever had a thought of moving on?'

'Can't say that I did. I fell into the work-life pattern here at Dukes, and that was it.'

Viola studied Ellis' body language. He was a man with no regrets for his decisions. She wished she had that level of satisfaction in her life, before she was too old and frail to appreciate life.

'I admire you for your loyalty and commitment, Ellis. It's a rare quality these days.'

'No different from what you do every day. I see your dedication to the job. Same thing, right? I wish you would set roots here.'

'Thank you, it's my restlessness, but one day...one day... hopefully soon.'

The conversation shifted to family, life, youth and change.

Viola relaxed after her unsettled start to the evening. She helped Ellis' lock-up and refused his offer to walk her back to her apartment.

She contemplated his peaceful nature, awed by how he hung onto that, but she knew he was hell-bent on bringing change to Blackwater Ridge. Her mood desired a space on the page.

> *the little things matter*
> *in a life well spent*
> *digging deep*
> *to quench the thirst for something new*
> *while old hidden charms*
> *surface, begging to be rediscovered*

Maud Cartwright delivered on her promise. Her niece was not returning that day. She called to pick her niece's brain on what she knew about the missing Blackwater Ridge young women. Maud's niece met Vivian in the park one morning while out for a run. She said she was a visitor passing through, and let on that she was staying at the campsite, a ten-minute drive from the park.

Andy hugged Maud for that bit of news. A live lead. Maud Cartwright emphasized her niece was adamant that the trapeze artist was a kind and caring man.

Sebastian and Andy headed to the campsite, hoping the young women were still there. The site was sparsely populated, except for three lonely tents on the far end of this silent lot.

'They've long gone, I tell you. They must be in Sydney by now. It might be worth talking to the people in those tents.'

Andy was not going back to Blackwater Ridge until he could bring Vivian home.

A laid-back atmosphere prevailed at this rural campsite. A lone figure on the pine tree facing side of the site puffed a pipe, sending billowing smoke trails snaking skywards. He stared out across at the cluster of pine trees. To the left of where he was seated, a woman stoked a fire with a steel pole and placed a blackened kettle on the flame. No children were around the tents. Old folk, retired folk, sat around shooting the breeze, staring out at the landscape, or nodding off to sleep. One active figure painted an interesting picture against this still, dry landscape. With his cowboy hat askance, the man threw a few darts on the board pinned to the tree trunk beside his tent. Sebastian watched him, fascinated by his obvious enjoyment in his solitary game.

'I'm heading over to chat to our cowboy dart player. He is the only moving target in this still landscape. He must know something.' Sebastian looked at Andy for approval.

'Do you know anything about the game?' Andy's dubious brow fired Sebastian to prove he did.

'I'll have ya know, mate, that I play the game at my local pub in NYC.'

'Aargh, quit the Aussie accent, please. Maud told you to get rid of it!'

Sebastian whistled and moseyed over to the man with a cheeky, backward glance at Andy. Both struck up a friendship in the first few hours on the road together.

'Good afternoon, there! You sure have a friendly game going all by your lonesome. Need some company?'

When the man spun around, it surprised Sebastian to see a youthful face – not a retiree, as he expected.

'Nah, I'm just whiling away me time, waiting for the missus to return with supplies she went to pick up. We're leaving in the morning.'

'That's a pity. I'm a mean hand at darts. Sure you don't want a few throws with me?'

'Here you go, have a throw.'

Sebastian snatched the opportunity and hit the bull's eye on the first shot.

'Wow-wee! Played like a pro! I hear your American accent as clear as day. Are you an international star dart player?'

'American, guilty as charged. A star, right off the mark there.'

'I'm Wayne Lombard. What's a guy like you doing in these parts? Nothing happening around here!'

'I'm helping a mate find his niece. She disappeared a week and a half ago. Joined some trapeze circus guy it seems.'

Wayne Lombard stopped his play and turned to face Sebastian with a quizzical look.

'Well, he was here for sure, over at that tent next to the white caravan. He left yesterday with two girls.'

'Two?'

'Yeah, two girls. Must have been his sisters. He took good care of them.'

'Did he look like a decent sort to you?'

'I think so, quiet type. Just nodded a greeting, never said a word. But you never know these days, do ya?'

'I'm walking over to check out the tent. Did anyone move into the caravan after he left?'

'Not sure.'

Sebastian motioned to Andy to follow him, and called out to the cowboy, 'This is my mate, the one I was telling you about.'

The caravan was a ramshackle old thing. As they got closer, the curtain on the back window drew apart and pulled together. A young woman ran out.

'Uncle Andy! How did you know where I was?'

Andy stared at Vivian in disbelief. She looked well, but stood a distance away, waiting for Andy's reaction.

'Vivian! Am I glad to see you! Your mother is ill with worry over your whereabouts. Why did you leave without a word?'

Vivian went from excited to see Andy to uncomfortable in a second! She glanced at Sebastian and back at her Uncle Andy.

Andy was quick to grab the moment.

'May I have a word with you in private? This is my friend Seb, from America. He has been helping me to find you. I'll tell him to give us some alone time.'

Sebastian smiled and walked away.

'Please promise you won't be angry with Rick. I left of my own choosing. He did not force me to do anything. He tried to persuade me to talk to a family member, but I was afraid they would yank me back. Please do not dob him to the police, please Uncle Andy.'

'I need your help to save your friends. You know I will take you back home with me.'

'I can't go back. Not now.'

'Why ever not?'

'Can't say... but I will help you find the others.'

'I need to get you into proper accommodation. Then you can call your mother to put her anxiety to rest.'

'Proper accommodation? Where? I can't call mum, just yet.'

'A friend who lives around here. You will have a clean bed, a shower, and some nutritious food. Sebastian is an ally. He can be trusted. For now, I will respect your wish not to speak to your mother, but you cannot expect me to withhold this for too long. Just so you know.'

A call to Maud confirmed she was happy to offer Vivian accommodation at her home. After Andy and Sebastian bundled her off to safety, they hit the road again in search of the other young women.

Andy could not honor Vivian's silence on being found. He called his wife to let her know Vivian was unharmed, but that she could not tell her brother just yet until Vivian was ready to do so herself. He needed another day or two off from the Academy, and Viola agreed. She wished she could be out on the road with them. Sebastian knew her special set of investigative skills would be handy right now, especially on her way with young people. Her leadership role pinned her to a loaded desk of responsibilities.

'This Rick, trapeze artist fellow seems to have his way into the girls' hearts. He can do nothing wrong, according to Vivian. Maud and her niece said much the same thing about him. Perhaps Vivian is telling the truth.'

'Is Blackwater Ridge such a dead, uninteresting place to youth that, at the first tinkling of adventure, they run off?' Sebastian asked.

'It appears so. Thank God they are unharmed. We feared what we would find when we came this way. You know this makes me think, I don't want to raise my family here, yet I was born and raised in town. I think I came out ok.'

'Different times, that's what it is.'

'You say that like an old man, Seb. You can't be over thirty yourself.'

'Something like that. It is a pleasant town with poor leadership, that's all. The place is crying for change, although I like the laid-back atmosphere of Blackwater Ridge, but it seems youngsters don't.'

Andy pondered what change would come to Blackwater Ridge. He feared what would happen once Viola left the Academy. She gave him hope. The town flowed in his veins. He married a Blackwater Ridge girl who had family ties to an old hard-working mining family. She would never turn her back on what her ancestors had built.

Sebastian suggested that an early morning start with Vivian to find Rick and the girls was the best course of action. After an indulgent oversized round of burgers and chips, they fell into a carbohydrate comatose sleep in the car.

The sun streamed in through the windscreen. Andy opened one eye and jumped up when he realized his cell phone was ringing somewhere on the floor of the car.

It was Maud.

Vivian left during the night. She was unwell after dinner, throwing up and complaining of nausea. When Maud asked if she could be pregnant, she flew into a rage and locked herself in the bedroom.

Someone picked Vivian up from Maud's place that night. Her bag of clothes — gone with her. She walked out the front door.

It was unlocked.

2 2

The Academy's board called an urgent meeting with Viola. They were ready to present options on the way forward on the school's permanent leadership after Rob's passing.

Lawrence Hargreaves arrived half an hour early and popped his head into Viola's office. His title and position gave him free access around the Academy when he visited. Her PA greeted him with a heaven-sent smile and continued with her work. She would bruise everybody else with her insistence that her boss was unavailable, period!

Hargreaves needed no invitation.

'Ah, Ms Bardo, it seems I caught you at the right moment. I'll come right in. I'll only take a minute of your precious time.'

He plonked himself in the seat in front of Viola and smiled the smile he stole from her PA.

This was Viola's first ever conversation with the infamous Lawrence Hargreaves. An email exchanged between them after Rob Dwyer's passing was their only communication.

Viola returned his smile, although uncomfortable that the formidable man was in her office.

'Good to see you Mr Hargreaves. What has brought you in earlier than expected this morning?'

'Yes. Er...I had something to discuss with you in private before the board meeting.'

'I hope everything is ok.'

'It is, but forewarned is best, for a good outcome for all.'

Viola detested a cat-and-mouse game. She raised her teacher eyebrow at Lawrence Hargreaves. Rob Dwyer mentioned the board's top down, hands off approach. They issued instructions, expected the moon and stars, but never followed up or offered support in any form. Praise did not feature on their agenda.

'May I get you a coffee, Mr Hargreaves?'

'Lawrence, please. I just need a few minutes of your time. I will decline the coffee, now. The board convened last week and will present you with another option if you could not accept the full-time principal's position.'

Viola's dry mouth signaled her tension. She was being cornered into a situation that might make her feel guilty for her decision. Was she being hooked into something from which she could not extricate herself? Both her passions had to be kept alive. Holding onto Lorenza's memory and vision for a better world had to be honored.

'This sounds serious. Should I brace myself for it?'

Lawrence Hargreaves smiled at Viola's reaction.

'Nothing to fear, my dear. You might quite like the suggestion. It is to consider sitting on the school board.'

'In an official role?'

'No, not chairperson, or any such thing. I intend to hold my position for a while longer.' He laughed. 'We value your dedication and skills and want to maintain our connection with you. Rob was on the mark, presenting you to us as he did.'

'Bless him.'

'I won't press you for a response now but hope you would

think it through and have your questions ready for the board to eradicate any doubts.'

Strategist! Viola thought.

'The board sits in twenty minutes, so I better be off in pursuit of that coffee you offered.'

'Thank you for your kind words, and forewarning, but things are up in the air with our missing student out there somewhere.'

'That's the point – your heart and soul are here. We need you! Please do not disappear on us. I understand your fondness for Rob has kept you here this long.'

'My respect for Rob came first...'

'Off course! I did not mean to blindside that. Rob was a highly respected educator. I will leave you to your work as I wander around Rob's beautiful rose garden.'

Lawrence walked away, his step stealthy. The Academy was his alma mater. He and Rob clashed on several suggestions on how the Academy should be run, but Rob's worth was valued beyond his resistance.

Viola yearned for Tempest's advice. Her father would declare it an opportunity not to be missed. The board members were of advanced years. Maida Halliwell, at eighty-five, was the only woman on the board. Rob referred to her as the sparkling jewel among them. She prompted most ideas which the board neglected to pursue. Viola wondered whether Maida was retiring, hence the offer that was about to be presented to her. This did not fit in with her plans. What if Tempest needed her to investigate a case?

Her allegiances were being tested.

* * *

ANDY AND SEB drove to Maud's, showered, and guzzled down a fresh brew of coffee and bacon and egg rolls.

'I did not expect Vivian to do a runner on us, you know,'
Maud complained. 'She seemed to think this was a passing
phase. She was ready to go back to her life. Andy, I hate to say it,
but she is in the family way. You must speak to your wife to find
out who the father is.'

'How can you be so sure she is pregnant? What if she just
had an upset tummy?'

'No, Andy, this is not me speculating, a woman knows.'

'Merciful God, I don't know how her family will react?
Blackwater Ridge is a small town with long-tendrils of secrets.
This cannot be hidden, and if the young man, the baby's father, is
found, who knows what his fate will be.'

'If he is indeed a *young* man,' Sebastian piped in.

'Not now, please.' Andy begged.

After breakfast, Andy and Sebastian searched the area
around Maud's place for some sign on whether Vivian left on
foot or by car. Maud wished she could help, but exhausted
truckers wanted a hot breakfast after being on the road all night.

* * *

VIOLA JOINED the board in the meeting room. Hargreaves gave
her a knowing nod. Maida Halliwell pulled her to sit next to her.
These were strangers to her during her part-time teaching days at
the Academy. The grace and favor they were annointing made
her uncomfortable.

After a round of coffee, muffins, and some light chatter,
Lawrence Hargreaves stood up. Twelve board members were
about to decree her verdict. She had to be strong and direct in her
response. If she chose, based on guilt for doing the right thing for
Rob, this would be her life sentence. To be at peace with herself,
she had to stay the course. Music and justice would take
precedence.

Lawrence addressed her with no shame that he had already

let her in on the board's offer. Rob's disdain for how the man operated made sense.

'Ms Bardo, we value your work highly, hence the board and I have two propositions for you. Are you ready to hear it?'

'Thank you. Please go ahead.'

Viola's cheeks burned. She wanted this over as soon as possible.

Not a cough or a shuffle passed through the room.

He presented the options, highlighting that the first was for her to stay on as permanent principal, with the promise that she would have an assistant to allow her to travel. She could be their first virtual leader whenever she was away.

'We guarantee full pay upon your acceptance of the position.'

Viola's scalp tightened. Goosebumps rose from her ankles to her thighs. This was a died and gone to heaven offer. Her inner voice cautioned that she would be on constant call. Before she had time to digest the offer, Lawrence Hargreaves continued.

'Should that not suit you, we offer you a position as a silent board member. We will consult you on grave matters pertaining to the running of the Academy. We will detail this in a formal document written by our appointed legal team. This holds a board member's paycheck and healthy travel allowance.'

Viola heard the harp and saw the angels circling overhead. She assumed that being on the board was a voluntary position, not a paid job. The Academy was the alma mater of all who sat on the broad. She believed they were giving back to the school community because they valued the education they received decades earlier. What was her reason other than her allegiance to Rob Dwyer?

Viola left the meeting with the promise that she would consider the options presented and return with her answer within forty-eight hours.

Her promise felt hollow against the offer.
Fate tested her commitment to her purpose.

2 3

Once Viola had news from Sebastian, she told Andy to take the week off to locate Vivian and extend his search for the other young women. Rob's dedicated casual staff were eager to secure a few more days of work. Teachers rarely took days off at Blackwater Ridge Academy, a dedicated staff put students first.

Viola thought through several ways in which she would present her response to the board. Matthew Soto was the only person who would give her the advice she needed to hear. Now she yearned to have him close. She pushed him away, and she hated herself for it. It seemed right, then. Pride had no place in her life. She had the power to heal the impasse between them. Lorenza's whispered words returned.

Never rely on a stranger, or a man you have just met, to guide your important decisions. Know your heart well enough to do the right thing for you. Grace will guide you.

Would she be letting go of Lorenza's wisdom, or memory, if she called Matthew? She knew her heart, and chances were that

140

she could regret the rest of her days if she did not solicit his opinion. Opinion only, that would honor Lorenza. But Viola knew herself well enough to understand that if Matthew's opinion did not align with hers, she risked being mortally wounded. Rob's passing solidified the need to bury pride. Never had she imagined Rob would not return to this unscripted thing called life. Two people she cherished – gone from her life, forever. Just memories left behind. Out like a brief candle. Every moment must matter, must count.

A text message to Matthew flew off into cyberspace.

He was back in Greece with seven hours' time difference between them. Enough time to play out the scenarios on what he might say. She knew how to fill every thinking space she had. Overthinking was her mother's criticism of her. 2 am in Athens bought her the think time she needed.

An immediate response from Matthew at that hour, surprised her. It sent her pulse racing.

Hello. Where are you? Not at work today?

Guilt was her first reaction. Her jaw tightened. Caught! She was using work time for a private matter. Her mother admonished such behavior among her peers. Viola heard her mother berating human weakness from the cradle to the day her parents divorced. Guilt, mother-induced-guilt, scalded such moments.

At work, but in need of advice from you on a matter. Why are you awake at this hour on your end?

His reply sent her heart into a heady spin.

Waiting to hear from you, keeps me awake every night.

She paused, her hands trembling on the keyboard.

Are you able to chat around 1 pm your time? Get some sleep now, Matthew. It's a weighty subject I need advice on.

No reply.

Her worst fears surfaced. She had imposed on him again and he was not letting her do it!

Ten minutes later he agreed to chat at 1 pm.

Now getting on with her workday juggled with thoughts of speaking to Matthew slowed her down. Her head and heart were at loggerheads, but now the heart overruled reason.

* * *

MAUD CARTWRIGHT CALLED Andy to say that her niece was at her place and willing to speak to him in person, alone.

Sebastian headed off to the lakeside. Maud gave Andy and her niece the privacy of her office. She popped in with apple pie and coffee and tiptoed out.

Maud's niece, a lanky twenty-something-year-old, could pass for one in her early teens.

'I'm Taylor Cartwright. I am sorry to hear that Vivian has disappeared again. Your family must be distressed.'

'Thank you for meeting me. Did you know Vivian well?'

'Not really. I saw her twice at the local park, and we sort of struck up a friendship.'

'Did she speak to you about the trapeze artist she was following? Nothing is off limits. I need to know everything she revealed. Do you know if he is her boyfriend?'

'Oh, I don't know any of that. But what I can say is that Rick is a caring and responsible person. If he is dating Vivian, your family has nothing to worry about. Cross my heart on that.'

Andy had planned on asking Taylor if she knew Vivian was

pregnant. Now it seemed inconsequential when finding Vivian took priority.

'See, Mr Andy, youngsters get bored in these rural parts and the excitement Rick Mantel offers is tempting, its everything one dreams of at that age. Fame, you know, the need to be recognized as having a super skill.'

Andy nodded. He knew that Blackwater Ridge offered zero thrills to the younger generation, but Vivian, leaving without a word again, spoke of something more. Perhaps Maud's suggestion that she was pregnant had a ring of truth. The question was whether Vivian knew Rick Mantel before she left Blackwater Ridge.

'Do you know whether the other young women who joined Rick Mantel have gone to Sydney?'

'I don't think so. I saw one of them at the lakeside motel when Rick asked me to meet him there.'

'Is he still at the motel?'

'I think so. One girl was with him when I went over.'

'Please tell me why he wanted to see you.'

'He said he needed a doctor and asked if I could recommend a reliable one, as I am familiar with the locals.'

'Who did you send him to?'

Andy felt fear take hold. Perhaps Vivian was ill.

'I told him the new Italian doctor close to Maud's place was good. I don't know if he went to him.'

'Please, Taylor, will you take me to the doctor? I must speak to him as soon as possible. He might not want to talk to me if I went to him on my own.'

'I can try. Jump into my car, I'll drive you there.'

Andy sent a message to Sebastian about the situation, and Taylor got jumpy.

'Please, just you and me, nobody else. I do not want to get into any trouble with the doctor or the police.'

'Nobody else, I promise. Let's hurry!'

* * *

PROMPTLY AT **8 PM**, Matthew called Viola. His impatience could not wait a minute more. She picked up her glass of gin in one hand and the ringing phone in the other. Her nerves had to be steadied for this call.

'Hi Matthew, you beat me to it by a second.'

'I could not risk having you change your mind.'

The barb in his words conveyed he had not forgiven her abrupt departure from Porto. She cleared her throat.

'You have little faith in me, and I don't blame you.'

'Let's not go into that. You needed advice. I am all yours.'

She knew she deserved his hot and cold attitude. That is how he perceived her.

'Thank you for everything that you did for Papa in Porto.'

'Placido has become a dear friend. I wish to keep him out of whatever goes on between us, please.'

Viola pressed her lips together. Her reiteration of her thanks felt stupid at that moment.

'Fair enough. This is a work-related matter I hope to sound with you. The board has offered me two options to stay on at the Academy.'

She heard his deep inhale and then a long silence.

'Matthew, are you there?'

'Yes, I am. Tell me your thoughts on the matter.'

He listened intently as she explained what the board presented to her.

'I see, both positions are for you to remain in a full-time capacity in Blackwater Ridge.'

'Not exactly, the board role is voluntary, I think.'

'What's your heart telling you about these options?'

'I wish Rob Dwyer were still around to allow me to come and go as I have been.'

'That is your answer, right from the heart. You want your freedom to come and go, correct?'

'Yes, so what do you think?'

'You cannot accept either, as each impedes your freedom.'

'Is that what you think is the sensible thing to do?'

'If you are seeking my opinion, you are unsure of what you want. Buy some time from the board to think this through properly.'

'I have thought it through. I must give my answer by tomorrow.'

'You want things as they were, right? You said that, now. Do what you yearn to do.'

Matthew knew her well. He was letting her take ownership of what she already knew.

'Yes, that's the way it has to be. Thank you, Matthew.'

Viola hung up, feeling foolish for asking for advice on what her heart had already known.

2 4

Viola's mother called during her moral crisis on whether she would be dishonoring Rob Dwyer if she left the Academy. Helena always called her daughter when she was at her lowest. It was as though she sensed Viola's problems through an umbilical radar that only worked on negative vibrations. Never once was it a feel-good call. Viola's back was up when Helen cooed her infamous line.

'It has been a long time since I heard from you. Everything ok? How is your principal position going? Enjoying it or fighting it?'

'Hello mother. Sorry for being absent, it has been a crazy, past few weeks. Rob Dwyer passed away. Did papa tell you?'

'Your father never tells me anything. You should know that by now. I am sorry to hear this. Do you plan to stay on, now?'

And thus, her mother hit the bull's eye like she always did.

'Yes, I have to decide on that soon.'

Her mother dived in, powered, rearing to go!

'What is there to decide? I hope this time you are not letting a great opportunity slip through your fingers.'

Viola strummed the familiar air violin she had mastered over the years whenever she heard her mother's rant about what she had to do.

'I will return to my former role and let someone more suitable take the reins.'

'Now you sound as hopeless as your father! What are the options?'

Viola felt a heaviness descend over her.

'It makes no difference, mother. I have decided. I do not want a board position and prefer to teach to be true to my calling.'

'Are you suggesting that you are turning down two offers from the Academy?'

'Mother, we might as well hang up, if you feel you know what's best for me.'

'Don't rush into things like your papa does.'

'I have not consulted with him on my decision. He would be happy with whatever I choose.'

Helena's silence was her irritation that Placido was the center of Viola's world. She had lost her daughter in her many marital wars.

'You will do as you please. That I know is your obstinate nature.'

'Then I am my mother's daughter.'

'You will look back with regret if you rush headlong into a decision.'

'How would you know that, mother, without walking in my shoes?'

Viola hated these conversations with Helena. Today she could not be quiet and allow her mother to ride over her.

'Look, I know what I want from life.'

'That sounds like Lorenza's influence.'

'Let it be, mother, please don't drag Lorenza's name into this!'

The bitterness between them continued to brew after many

counseling sessions in the earlier years. With maturity, Viola let it pass. Today they were dangerously close to putting down the phone on each other – for good!

Helena did as she pleased. Placido's mild-mannered ways grated on her adventurous spirit until her infidelity ended their marriage. Now she was partying every weekend, entering dance competitions, and doing everything that was absent in her life with Placido Bardo.

'So, you will continue to pursue an exchange teacher role. Something that is for beginning teachers, not a woman in her forties.'

'I am going to ignore that comment altogether, mother.'

'I don't want to be the one saying, *I told you so*, when you realize what time wasted has done, or rather hasn't done.'

'You won't have to. Now, how about you, tell me what you have been up to these days?'

That was the invitation Helena needed to swoop in to rattle on about her dancing accolades, academic success, blah blah blah.

Viola's energy had dried up by the end of the conversation, and she was none the wiser. She mastered how to brush off the negativity Helena exuded, but there was a sting in some of her chastisements. Without a doubt, her mother's next call would be to jack Placido up for not guiding his daughter's decisions.

Viola sat in front of her laptop, relieved when the lines she typed spoke her truth...

It is with deep regret that I decline both your generous offers proposed. Thank you for your trust, and the opportunity to lead such a dynamic and respected institution...

Those wonderful words, *it is with deep regret,* gave her back the life she desired. She could go wherever she wanted to and do as she pleased. A message to Matthew followed.

I did it! I declined both offers, and might head back to Porto sooner than I expected.

His one-word response gave nothing away on the song she expected to hear and feel.

Congratulations

The words stared up at her, its heart hidden.
Then almost as if Mathew had read her thoughts another message followed.

Will call you soon. You have done well!

That was all she needed today. Sebastian, too, would support her decision. Tempest, she knew, would remain silent if asked for advice on her teaching career.

* * *

ON THE OUTSKIRTS OF TOWN, Andy caught up with the elusive Rick Mantel, trapeze artist extraordinaire, with a penchant for luring young women into his team. When Andy called out to him as he exited the motel, he hastened his steps. He stopped and turned to face Andy when he threw in that he was Vivian's uncle.

'She's here, and welcome to leave. Nobody stays against their will in my team.'

Rick's lithe body stiffened. He expected abuse and accusation from Andy.

'May I speak with her?'

'Yeah, wait here, but be warned, she is unwell and under medical care which we arranged late last night.'

'We?'

'My team and I, we are a supportive, caring group.'

Andy waited in reception while Rick called one of the young women to escort Vivian to the foyer.

She was pale, unsmiling, her hair unkempt.

'I knew you would find me, Uncle Andy. Can we please talk in the car?'

Rick left them at the car and whispered something to Vivian. Andy saw the ease of their friendship.

'What did Rick say to you?'

'Nothing except that he would wait in the foyer, and to call him if I felt stressed talking to you.'

'I have one question. Are you pregnant? If so, who is the father?'

Andy did not expect Vivian's strong-willed disposition to crack with that question. She put her hands over her face and sobbed from a place deep inside her.

'I am, and please don't think Rick is the father, he's not. He's like a big brother to me and the others.'

'Are you sure you're not just saying that to protect him?'

'No, I'm not! You don't know the half of it!'

'Tell me, help me understand.'

'I don't want to talk about it now.'

Andy pulled back. He had to keep Vivian happy to gain her trust, if he was to persuade her to return home with him.

'As you will. Where are the other girls?'

'Here, except for one who left for Sydney.'

'May I speak with those who are here? My friend Seb will arrive shortly. He has my absolute trust in all matters.'

'Yeah, sure, the truth is out, anyway. No point hiding it now.'

Sebastian waited in the motel foyer with Rick Mantel. The girls strolled in after Vivian called them. Tamarind Jenkins, the Academy's missing student, was one of them. The older looking young woman cowered behind Tamarind.

Vivian took the lead. Her courage returned with a mercurial

shift. She hooked her arm through Tamarind's. The girl was petrified, with schoolmaster Andy looking at her. The older girl introduced herself as Phoebe Constantine. Andy had never seen her before in Blackwater Ridge. She said she was new in town and a TAFE student. She addressed Andy and Sebastian.

'I am really sorry you had to come out all this way looking for us. Our loved ones must be stressed with our sudden, unexplained departure. I am not sure if my family in Tasmania know anything about this. I lead my own life and, moved to Blackwater Ridge six months ago. I'm ready to return to finish my studies. I don't hack it as a gymnast, but I'm glad I tried though.'

Tamarind nodded with her eyes fixed to the floor.

'Can anyone tell me where in Sydney might we locate, Milsom Jones' granddaughter?' Andy asked.

'Nadia said she would never return to Blackwater Ridge when we heard you were out looking for us. She is not answering our calls,' Tamarind whispered without making eye contact with Andy.

'Rick, do you know where she is?'

'She left without saying a word. I do not know where she is.'

Sebastian stood up. He had enough with the diversions and circuitous questions and answers.

'You know we are not forcing you to return with us to Blackwater Ridge. Just so that you understand that the choice is yours. Remember, we must report the matter to the police commissioner. He will ask you to make a statement to clear Rick, as he might deem him the alleged kidnapper in this situation. We are heading back this afternoon. Who wishes to return?'

Phoebe and Tamarind nodded.

'Rick did not kidnap us. We responded to his recruitment advertisement,' Phoebe clarified.

'What about you, Vivian?' Andy asked.

'If I can stay at your place with Aunt Philipa for a few days before I see my mother, then I will.'

'Done! Good!' Andy hoped this decision would not court disfavor from his in-laws.

Sebastian said, 'Rick, would you be willing to return to Blackwater Ridge with us to clear this up?'

'I don't want to be held responsible for Nadia leaving. Yes, I have nothing to hide. I will follow you back to town.'

Andy sighed, relieved, and grateful for Seb's firm stance on what the expectation would be upon arrival in Blackwater Ridge.

2 5

A second letter arrived from Tempest's lawyer, instructing Viola to set up a video call with Sebastian present.

After more than three years as Tempest's vigilante agent, the doyenne was about to become a face, not just a husky, caramel-toned voice. Sebastian had only been on one case with her before the Blackwater Ridge problem. Why did she want a video call after all this time? Viola enjoyed the mystery of Tempest's presence in her life. That was soon ending. The letter informed that the call would be from Tempest's hospital bed with her medical specialist and lawyer present.

This was serious business, and Viola felt a pang of concern that perhaps Tempest was more ill than she had let on. She was edgy and her sugar craving kicked in like she had not put it on hold! The old peanut brittle urge was dominant now, but it would trigger dizzy spells and a muzzy head. She needed clarity for this historical video call. To calm her nervous energy, she prepared a batch of peanut brittle, but promised herself it was for her staff morning tea. She would not eat a morsel. The aroma fed her craving. As she stirred the rapidly hardening caramel glug, she pondered why Tempest was revealing herself now. She swung from elation to despair, and a night of sleeplessness followed. Before her alarm went off, she bolted out of bed and hopped into her tracksuit. A jog on the beach promised the energy she needed for the day ahead. Sleeplessness was a feature of her life ever since she assumed Rob's role. She reminded herself it was temporary to survive the days that tested her patience, strength, and clarity.

It was dark at 4:30 am on the beach strip. A lone figure sat on the sea facing bench. The woman turned when she heard footsteps and caught sight of Viola running. Under her breath she whispered, 'Another one having a restless night... what's your story then? My muse left me. You know what that is like?'

A few residents in Blackwater Ridge struggled with loneliness. Isolation and perceived failed dreams haunted their nights. Viola raised her hand in greeting but said nothing as she jogged past the woman.

At the water's edge, she pulled off her hoodie, unpinned her hair and tossed her head skywards to allow the chilly morning air to pass through her locks. She drew three deep inhalations and felt instantly calm. White foaming cotton wool waves were a comforting sight. Tears rolled down her face as the cold air lashed against her cheeks. She ran the length of the beach and turned to make her way back to her apartment before the sun drove the darkness out. Hers eyes were moist, her hair wild, and her nose cherry red. Now was not the time to be seen by staff or students. She tightened her hoodie under her chin and bounded back to her place.

She avoided Dukes and headed to the Academy an hour earlier than usual. Music beckoned – the piano sat forlornly in the corner of her old music space. The temporary teacher played drums and guitar and a bit of saxophone, not piano. Viola dusted down the lid, lifted it and played soothing melodies she knew as second nature. Lorenza loved watching her play and encouraged her passion for music. After Lorenza's disappearance and Tempest's arrival in her world, her enthusiasm for piano playing returned. Unreachable and incapable of communicating without her doctor and lawyer was not how Viola had expected to see Tempest for the first time. She romanticized about visiting Tempest in an old castle one day, somewhere in a hidden part of the world. Water was always in those visions. Now the unknown was beckoning, throwing her off kilter. Was she ready to face the mysterious Tempest she was in awe of?

She stopped when she heard voices outside. Staff and students were arriving for the day! The door flung open.

'Oh, it's you, Ms Bardo, good morning. I'm so sorry. I did not expect to find you in here. When students said they heard music wafting across the oval, I thought an intruder had entered the building. So sorry to disturb you.'

'I should say sorry for intruding on this space. I came in early and decided to tinker on the piano a bit. I miss it, you know.'

'Ah, you play so beautifully. I remember the assemblies when Mr Dwyer would ask you to play.'

Nostalgia kicked Viola in the guts.

'Beautiful memories! Now to work I go! Have a good day.'

Viola hurried off to her office amidst eager greetings from students who had congregated around the music room.

Andy was due back in the classroom tomorrow. Viola was keen for first-hand news from him. Her day passed in a whimsical swirl and she caught herself humming the tunes she played that morning.

Sebastian received her message that it was imperative that they meet as soon as he was back in Blackwater Ridge.

Viola stopped at Duke's around six o'clock. Ellis' broad smile welcomed her.

'Thought you had forsaken Dukes when I didn't see you this morning.' He chuckled.

'Never! This is my haven, my second home. I think of you as family, Ellis.'

'Thats good to know, likewise, my dear. Everything ok today? I missed your cheery self this morning.'

'I think so, although I will be happy once my student is back home. I will chat to Andy on the latest news this evening.'

'I do know Andy's located his wife's niece.'

Ellis knew a lot more about what transpired with the missing girls, but he left it to Andy, to fill her in.

'Good to know. Hopefully, this will soon be behind us with all concerned, happy with the outcome.'

'One hopes for that. What can I get you, I have freshly baked chicken pies and steamy pepper gravy?'

'I'm sold, chicken pie and gravy it is!'

After a hearty meal with a dear friend, Viola went home to call Sebastian with the news from Tempest's lawyer. Sebastian sounded like he was out walking when he picked up her call.

'Hi there, did I call at an awkward time?'

'Viola! Gosh it is good to hear your voice. I forgot to deactivate this number, but it's a good thing, at least you could reach me. I'm good to chat. What's on your mind?'

'Any further updates on the girls? Ellis mentioned Andy had some success in finding his niece.'

'Indeed, we have. I needed a bit of a walk before I called to tell you.'

'Tell me. I am bursting to know.'

'We have three of them. We planned to return to Blackwater Ridge this afternoon but decided tomorrow mid-morning would be best.'

'Stop toying with me. Tell me who you found and where are they now? I guess Andy won't be in at the Academy tomorrow. I will arrange casual staff for the day.'

'He might have forgotten to inform you with all he has to put up with. Tamarind Jenkins has been located. It will please you to know, and the other young woman I only remember her last name, Constantine, that's terrible of me! The worrying thing is that Milsom's granddaughter has gone to Sydney and nobody knows where exactly.'

'Thank God, Tamarind is ok, I wish you told me that earlier, but it's a concern that Milsom's granddaughter ran off again. How is Andy doing? Is his niece willing to return to Blackwater Ridge?'

'It's far from over. There is one problem, if we can label it as a *problem*. Vivian's pregnant.'

'Good grief, poor Andy! He will have to explain it to his in-laws, and from what little I know of them, they are not amiable people. Family name and honor stuff, you get it? Typical town mindset.'

'She wants to stay at his place until she's ready for her mother to know her situation.'

'Is the trapeze guy the father?'

'She says he's not, but won't name the father.'

'Well, what do you know, Blackwater Ridge is not so still, after all?'

'Are you able to ask Ellis to schedule a meeting for Andy with Mayor Corey tomorrow afternoon?'

'It's a brief notice, but if anyone can get around, Corey, it's Ellis.'

'Thank you for that. I look forward to catching up with you tomorrow. Shall we meet for dinner at Dukes?'

'It's better we meet here at my place. I'll prepare dinner.'

It did not feel right to casually mention that Tempest requested a video call. This had to be a face-to-face conversation. Sebastian would be awkward with seeing Tempest in a hospital bed.

26

Mayor Corey's me, myself, and I headquarter declined Andy's request for a meeting because the mayor's office was rather busy. The police commissioner was keen to meet, but Corey's power halted that.

Viola struggled to comprehend how someone like Corey, lacking in charisma and moral mettle, could silence a town. His oratory skills left much to be desired, and yet he had key personnel in town at his beck-and-call. When Ellis called Viola, he was irate with Corey's obstinance. She marched down to the mayoral building to give him a piece of her mind. For all his resistance, his office was the easiest to enter. His doors were open, but the secret, incarcerated in his mind and soul were impenetrable.

'Good day, Mayor Corey. I apologize for barging in, but we have urgent matters to attend to, such as the safe return of our missing young women to the town's social and family hub. I have it on good authority that Milsom Jones' granddaughter has not been located and is allegedly somewhere in Sydney. Regarding the upstanding Milsoms, you owe it to Andy to hear him out on what he has unearthed. It is your moral obligation to take an interest in and action a successful conclusion to this situation. You must allow the search for Nadia. We do not know where she is and whether she is in danger.'

Mayor Corey stood up slowly. Age groaned in his joints, but his eyes sparkled with smugness.

'I understand your concern, but we must not overreact to that we do not know or understand. You said, *allegedly* in Sydney. There you have it. There is nothing we can do until we have hard evidence.'

This incredulous man, responsible for a town of good people, ignored all but one word of what she said.

'By *hard*, what are you suggesting, a dead body? Please explain your understanding to me.'

The teacher kicked in. Corey would not get away with implausible suggestions.

His silence provoked her unreserved irritation.

'As acting principal at the Academy, I have a student who is caught up in this foray, and Rob Dwyer would expect me to see justice served. I am calling the metropolitan police to put out an APB on Nadia Jones.'

Blood surged to Viola's head, and a brief, dizzy spell stopped her tirade.

Nobody had ever challenged Corey. He never expected the soft-spoken Ms Bardo to be a firebrand ready to crucify him. From under his bushy eyebrows, he fixed a menacing look at her.

'That would not be wise, Ms Bardo. Leave me to run this town, and you go back to leading the Academy.'

Viola's voice, several decibels lower, whispered to freeze hell over.

'Wise? Did you say wise, Mayor Corey? Wise for you, not the young women who kept this town sleepless from the day they disappeared. If we do not address this now, we will have more of this happening. I ask you, is that wise?'

She had said all she had to say. There was nothing to lose. Soon she would vacate her position at the Academy. They would not silence her. Tempest would expect that of her, and Lorenza would applaud somewhere.

'Thank you for your time, Mayor Corey.'

Viola walked out of the insufferable mayor's office, trying to keep her dignity intact.

* * *

ANDY AND SEBASTIAN returned with Vivian, Phoebe, and Tamarind. Nadia Jones had dropped off their radar. Vivian was safely ensconced with Andy's wife. Her return home had to be carefully processed. Andy asked Viola to speak to Vivian about her situation. She refused to get involved in family matters but softened when Ellis pleaded with her to get Vivian to tell her the narrative of her situation. Ellis provided his office space at Dukes for their meeting. Viola and Vivian entered the office from the laneway behind the building. There were always unseen eyes watching and ears ready to grab an airwave ripe with gossip. Small town in need of denied excitement. Ellis locked the door inside Dukes to prevent unsanctioned access. People freely came into his office seeking advice or when needing a listening ear. Such was Ellis' commitment to serving his community.

Viola locked the laneway entrance door behind her as soon as Vivian entered.

'Thank you for meeting me, Vivian. Are you comfortable telling me everything about your departure from the town? Why you did it and who is the father of your unborn child?'

'I prefer to speak to you because you understand young people more than anyone else in this town. The question my parents would want answered is the same as you ask, but their reaction is what I fear the most.'

'Thank you for trusting me. I will let you speak uninterrupted and ask further questions at the end, if I have any to ask by then.'

Vivian spoke with confidence and a maturity quite unlike other young people her age in Blackwater Ridge.

'I have not had a pregnancy test, but my swelling belly and bouts of nausea confirm I am. I want to clarify that Rick Mantel is not the father. I left when I realized I was pregnant. My situation is scandalous in this town. My parents might disown me, who knows.'

Viola knew Vivian was as honest as she could be.

'I spent a night with the drummer who plays at Dukes on a Friday night.'

Viola rarely attended the late night Friday gigs at Dukes and looked at Vivian, confused.

'You might not know him. It's Spenser Corey.'

Viola frowned and could not help asking after promising not to interrupt.

'Mayor Corey's nephew?'

'Yes, I know he is much older than I am. We struck up a friendship over a few months, both needing a listening ear. He has no idea I'm pregnant, and I have no intention of telling him. I guess the rest is history.'

Viola did not expect to hear this piece of information. Now she held the secret that only Vivian knew.

They sat in silence for a few seconds before Viola spoke.

'I take it you won't be telling your parents any of what you have just told me.'

'I will tell them I'm pregnant, but not about Spenser. I don't want a commitment from him, or to make him feel responsible.'

Viola heard the voice of Blackwater Ridge's breakaway generation in Vivian's words. Change was here and Vivian's parents, Corey et al., had to brace themselves for it.

'Whatever you choose to do is up to you. Something obviously set your mind on how to proceed with this. I will let your Uncle Andy know, but I will not mention Spenser Corey. I'll leave that to you.'

'Thank you, Ms Bardo. I knew I could trust you. Please don't tell him Spenser is the father.'

'Spenser has a right to know, just as you have a right not to take the relationship to the next level.'

'I know, but I'm not ready to tell him yet.'

'Fair enough.'

Vivian left Ellis' office and ten minutes later Andy and Sebastian arrived with Ellis following. Viola felt the weight of harboring this secret.

All three men looked at her, expecting the Niagara to gush.

'All I can say is that if Vivian is pregnant, the trapeze guy, Rick is not the father.'

'That's it?' Andy asked, 'is that all she said for half an hour?'

'It's up to her when she tells her family. I have nothing more to say.'

Andy paced the small space, agitated that Viola was tight-lipped.

'I counted on you finding out more. I am back at the same point. Why?'

'She asked for my trust. I will not breach that. Vivian will speak to you about what she told me.'

'Sanctimonious bullshit!'

'I beg your pardon, Andy!'

This was the first time in all the years that they had worked together on and off that both lost their cool with each other.

Sebastian stepped in with a shocked Ellis watching on.

'Get some rest, Andy. It has been a trying few days. Vivian will come around. She trusts you. I've seen that.'

Andy stormed out of Ellis' office.

'He will simmer down, I promise. He wants this over as much as we do.'

'Have the other two young women been reunited with their families?'

'Yes, the police commissioner took their statements without Corey's permission, finally, and delivered Tamarind to her family. Phoebe is Tasmanian, she lives in the old couples' share house next door to Milsom Jones.'

Ellis listened, knowing that his town was far from over this.

Viola thanked him for the office space and left with Sebastian lightening the mood.

'I'll be here, bright and early, for my usual feed tomorrow morning, Ellis!'

'See you then, Seb,' a tired Ellis replied.

Viola and Sebastian walked back to her apartment. Her pensive mood unsettled him.

'Will you fill Ellis in on what Vivian revealed?'

'No, it's not my place to say anything to anyone.'

'I take it. I'm also barred from knowing.'

'You bet your bottom dollar! And don't say I'm a true-blue Blackwater Ridge townsfolk resident now!'

Her somber tone stopped Sebastian's prying. If there was something he valued in Viola, it was her unquestionable trust.

The truth Sebastian needed to know was that Tempest requested a video call.

'Tempest's lawyer is holding a video meeting, and we are summoned to be present.'

'Lawyer? What's going on?'

'As we suspected, Tempest has been unwell for some time. Her lawyer has been in contact with me regarding what he said was minor surgery. I assume it's more than they have led us to believe. She will speak to us early next week.'

'Jeez, much has happened in a few days. I'm available anytime. How about you?'

'I will fit in with whatever is requested to ensure Tempest is satisfied.'

'Just when you think you have everything under control, along comes something else.'

Viola stared at him, concerned that he might see her as a guardian of secrets.

'It's a relief to know, Tamarind is back, but the Milsoms are having a rough time figuring out why Nadia chose not to return home with the others. How I wish I could head off to Sydney and find her myself.'

2 7

The mayor stayed home the day after the three young women returned to Blackwater Ridge – his front door double bolted, and his curtains drawn. His office was closed for the first time in as many years as he served in the role. The young women returned willingly after feeling the pinch of a hard life on the road as novice gymnasts searching for a sense of self.

Cesario Lane Bakery was shut. People loitered outside, hoping the bakery would open for their customary purchases of fresh bread. Milsom Jones' family isolated themselves, devastated that Nadia did not return with the others. Viola knew there were issues with Nadia's parents' divorce, which made it impossible for her to intervene as a friend, to ease the family's pain. Nadia's struggle was Viola's lived memory, but her position and title closed her off from reaching out on personal matters. It was no surprise that Nadia might have headed to Sydney. She was raised there until her parents' divorce a year ago. Viola had success in gaining support from one officer at the metro station. He said Nadia was eighteen, which made it difficult to force her to return, but he would put out a watch for her.

Viola yearned to tap into Tempest's contacts to speed up the process. Tamarind and Nadia troubled her. They were similar in age and temperament, yet Tamarind returned. The consequences were dire for school going Tamarind, but she returned to face the music. The police commissioner said he would place her on community service for two weeks if Mayor Corey approved.

Viola's reliance on Tempest was second nature. Now she regretted not coercing Tempest to talk about herself. The mystery was Tempest's and only she could open the door to what she chose to reveal – her superpower that drew Viola into her mission.

The Academy had to run smoothly without ruffling parents and students. Maintaining calm was imperative for learning, and a smooth hoped for exit for Viola from the role. Questions would haunt Tamarind from both students and a nosey parent community. Viola warned staff not to talk to her about the situation.

Ellis was uneasy, quite out of character for the good man who did his due diligence by visiting Milsom at home. Andy retuned to the Academy, guilty for his outburst the day before. Viola exercised good judgement and refrained from raising the issue. He promised himself he would apologize to Viola when the time was right. His sister-in-law had to manage her daughter's issues. He had done his part and had to go on with his life without destroying the friendships he cherished.

* * *

THREE DAYS after Sebastian's return, Tempest's lawyer set up the date and time for their much-awaited video call. His broad questions appeared to be a formality to prevent him from being sued for any matter deemed inappropriate. The first was whether Viola and Sebastian were comfortable talking live via video to Tempest from her hospital bed. The second stipulation was whether her ill-health and dependence on an oxygen tank during their meeting would be a point of distress for either of them.

The third point – a dagger to Viola's heart asked if talking about Lorenza was off limits? Lorenza? Why? This had nothing to do with her. Viola wondered how Sebastian would feel about such a question when it was unrelated to him. Small print at the bottom of the page stated: *Sensitivity to divorce and adoption should be lodged in writing in reply to this email.* The last line mentioned additional time and availability — should Tempest feel exhausted during the call, would they accept a rescheduling of the meeting?

Viola's anxiety brewed over so many matters of late, but this made her nervous. It sounded as though Tempest was gravely ill, and finalizing things.

Sebastian reviewed the questions before Viola responded to the email.

'This seems vague. Why are family issues being dragged in? It feels more like Tempest making her exist.'

'Do you mean she's dying? I fear that so much.'

'No! Relinquishing her vigilante leadership position is what I meant. Maybe you are going to be the new Tempest! Let me see, what would be your new name?'

'This is no time to joke around, Sebastian. Don't you dare give me some strange or idiotic name!'

'I wouldn't dare to do that.'

Viola knew he was itching to tease her with some stormy name.

'Anyway, we are her agents on the ground, and so we shall remain.'

Unstrung thoughts hung over them.

Finally, Viola broke into their silence.

'The Academy's board has not responded to my letter declining the roles they offered me. I said I can only stay on until they appointed a replacement.'

'Did you give them a cut-off date on that? They could string you along until the end of the year if you are not forthright with them.'

'I said only six weeks from my refusal to their offer. '

'Good, that is a generous time frame. Only you would do that.'

'So, you would not have done the same? I am surprised.'

'Nope! I would not give a minute more once my contract ended.'

Viola cast Sebastian a dubious look. Was he being that cheeky littler brother she thought he was when they met in Athens, or was he capable of being this hard?

'Stop overthinking this. I can see that furrowed million-miles-away look on your face.'

'Now you sound like Helena! I do not need another mother!'

Before they knew it, it was well past midnight. They were both drained from revisiting the questions too many times.

'Would you mind if I crashed on your couch tonight?'

'Don't do this to me, Sebastian. What if Ellis, Corey, or the school board get wind that you are staying over at my place? This is a small town.'

'Why does it have to be unacceptable or wrong? We are friends. The town thinks we met a few days ago.'

'That makes it all the worse. We apparently barely know each other. It's a small town, not New York!'

'Got it! I'm leaving, Ms Proper, sorry Ms Bardo.'

'That's mean, but it is best you go back to your motel.'

'Yes, and what if some town big shot sees me leaving now? Anyway, I'm out of here. Get some sleep. You have work in the morning while I sleep in.'

He grinned, bowed, and left.

She knew he would be asleep the minute his head hit the pillow and she would count sheep until the sun came up. Leadership came at a price; she could not call in sick for a mental health day.

Soon this will be behind her.

With sleeplessness, poetry filled her mind. Viola picked up her phone and dictated the lines that toyed with her thoughts.

crime now not a crime
half solved – one to be found
elusive Tempest soon a naked babe
an enigma seen with fresh eyes
her caramel tones soothe
is she old, is she tall?
where is she now?
and what of Lorenza
will she return from the heart's grave?
to save her brother and bring joy
back to our lives
oh patience that necessary evil
suspends sleepless nights
surmising
between a sleeping-waking state

Richard Monroe and Associates, representing Tempest, proposed the video meeting for Saturday. Viola knew Tempest had a hand in the choice of day, not to disrupt her work life. Sebastian was happy to book in the earliest day possible and agreed to meet at Viola's apartment on the allotted day. He was curious why this time Tempest's call was during Blackwater Ridge's daylight hours, the early afternoon, when her previous calls were late at night or early in the morning.

Viola took a run on the beach at 5 am that morning. The night before she tossed aside her paperwork and busied herself spring cleaning her apartment down to clearing out her fridge. She avoided food with the queasiness, anxiety brought, and downed coffee and crackers. Anxiety played havoc with her tummy ever since she was a child. Her mother put it down to a colon issue. She diagnosed all Viola's ailments based on everything, except her lack of emotional connection.

Sebastian arrived at 3 pm with a box of six fresh cream donuts and a tray of sausage rolls. He devoured pastry and sugar when he was nervous.

'Do you have some of the red wine we shared the other night, when you kicked me out.' He winked at a tense Viola.

'We are not having a booze-up before we speak to Tempest. She may be unwell but never fear, she is razor sharp on detecting unprofessionalism.'

'So, is this a professional call? It sounded like her lawyer proposed a personal call, in dragging your family into whatever she has to say. Then a no wine afternoon it shall be!'

'What's with these decadent treats, it's not like Tempest is coming over.'

'Sorry, I don't have peanut brittle! I wish Tempest were coming over. I need these treats to calm my nerves. Are you as tense as I am?'

'Gin would be my choice, but I need a clear head.'

Sebastian walked over to the gin bottle and mimicked pouring a shot, then handed her an empty glass.

'For you, madam! Enjoy!'

Viola had to smile at Sebastian's boyish antics. He had a way of lightening her moments.

They waited in the Zoom holding space, nervously expecting Tempest's appearance.

Sebastian passed Viola a sausage roll. She declined.

'Be a good lad and pour me a mug of coffee, please.'

'Sure! Would madam like anything else?'

'Stop it, Sebastian. We need to be serious. Tempest might pop in any minute now.'

'Serious stuff. Look at you dressed in a suit on a Saturday afternoon!'

'I need some quiet time, please.'

He put his fingers to his lips and slipped into the kitchen on tiptoe to pour her a mug of filtered coffee. She leaned forward, staring at her laptop screen.

At 4 pm, her screen lit up, and the image cleared. It transported them to a hospital room. On a raised bed a woman's face surrounded by thick, spiraled curls stared back at them. An oxygen mask affixed across her mouth. She raised her hand, and the doctor beside her removed the mask.

A soft caramel toned voice said, 'Sebastian, Viola, oh at last.'

She heaved, and her doctor placed the mask back on her face.

Viola' emotions threatened to erupt. This was the first time she heard Tempest's fondness for her agents. She held back her tears.

Sebastian reacted first.

'Tempest, how wonderful to see you, after all this time. I wish under better circumstances, though.'

'How are you, Tempest?' A subdued Viola asked.

The doctor popped his head onto the screen.

'Good afternoon, Viola and Sebastian. Tempest tires easily and will speak in brief spurts. She will type some of her conversation with you. Please scroll through the message section. I hope this will not be distressing for you.'

Both chorused, 'Not at all.'

'Whatever is best to keep Tempest comfortable, we're happy to oblige.'

Tempest typed, asking about the case of the missing young women, and congratulated Sebastian on his work with Andy.

Then she spoke again in her husky, lowered tone.

'I will have someone follow up on the girl who did not return.'

She typed she was sorry for being absent and cautioned both to take great care of their wellness.

Never neglect your health for anything or look at what happens.

She raised her eyebrows.

'Rest Tempest. We could talk again later,' Viola said.

Tempest raised her hand in protest and spoke.

'I'm good for now. I have some important things to say. Read carefully as I type.'

How is your father, Viola?

Viola replied, 'Placido is good. Thank you for asking.'

Brace yourself for this. I met your Aunt Lorenza before she went into hiding.

 Viola put her hand to her mouth to stifle her gasp.

It is because of her I contacted you.

'How? Is she alive? Where is she?'

One thing, at a time my dear. Unknown to you and your father, a man with underworld connections blackmailed Lorenza to get close to your father. When she refused to do as he asked her, he threatened to kill her family.

Uncontrollable tears ran down Viola's face. Sebastian moved closer and touched her arm.

What I have to say is going to shock, hurt, and challenge you. Are you prepared for the truth? It is never easy to hear the past return when you have reached a level of acceptance that it has passed.

'Please, just say it,' Viola sobbed.

I did not hear your response to that, Sebastian.

'I am ready to hear the truth you have to share, Tempest.'
Tempest paused.
The doctor stepped in to adjust her oxygen mask. Then another figure, her lawyer, sat at the side of her bed.

This is .... Richard of *Richard Monroe and Associates.*

Richard nodded.

My bother Bernado was a vigilante fighter against a global underworld syndicate. He placed Lorenza in my care for a few days before he moved her to a safe house. In an altercation with the man who threatened Lorenza, he fired a fatal shot. Bernado was in jail all these years and died late last year.

'Where is Lorenza now?'

That I cannot answer. My brother took that secret to his grave.

Viola stood up, agitated, pacing, swinging her arms around to release the tense stiffness in her neck.
'Dear merciful God, she might be safe, or heaven forbid, dead somewhere. How do I tell my father this news?'

Say nothing to him just yet. I need to rest for a while. Are you able to continue in two hours?

The doctor popped his head in front of Tempest.
'If you are available, Tempest's lawyer will call you back.'
'We will wait,' Sebastian said, looking at Viola for approval.
'Yes, we will.'
The screen clicked off.
A black screen with their silhouetted heads and shoulders stared back at them.

Viola put her face in her hands, bent over and sobbed like a child drawing from where many years of anguish lay buried.

She was inconsolable.

Sebastian rubbed her back, careful not to say anything that would upset her more.

'I did not expect to hear that. My head is a mess. How will I ever tell papa what I just heard? For so long, we waited for someone to shed some light on what happened to Lorenza. I convinced myself that she was safe and hopefully happy. I was at peace with that. Now this! I am worse off for hearing it.'

Sebastian knew Viola to be a strong woman, the only one he had ever met. Now her heart was shattered.

'I can only imagine the pain you feel. Why would Tempest reopen that wound? There is more that is unsaid.'

'I don't know if I'm up to hearing more. She will be back in two hours.'

'We should go out for a walk.'

'I can't go anywhere. You go out if you want a walk.'

'I won't leave you alone. May I play some music to soothe you?'

'Thank you. I prefer that.'

Viola curled in a tiny ball on the couch, fearing the worst was yet to come. Sebastian threw a rug over her as soft classical piano sounds wafted across the room.

Tempest was the oracle, but the hardest part for Viola would be telling her father. All she had, was one piece of the puzzle. She had never lied to Placido. Now things were different. His ailing health did not make telling him this truth possible.

A disconcerting mood crept over Sebastian. What was he to hear about his life? He wanted to believe nothing could be worse than the childhood he endured in his constant quest to belong.

29

Tamarind Jenkins was still on a break from the Academy. She called Viola in the middle of the school day.

Maida Halliwell was in a meeting with Viola in her last-ditch attempt to persuade her to take on at least one offer from the board. Her plea was that the community needed her fresh blood, and that she settle down and start a family in Blackwater Ridge. Tamarind's call was well-timed to end Maida's persistence.

Viola took her urgent call in an adjoining office.

'Hello, Viola Bardo speaking. Is that you, Tamarind?'

'Yes, it is. Thank you for taking my call.'

'I am relieved to hear from you. Are you planning on returning to school? You do know you need the police commissioner's permission to return while the investigation is going on regarding Nadia Jones.'

'I'm sorry to barge into your busy day. You are the only one I trust to speak to about Nadia.'

The hairs on Viola's arms and neck prickled.

'Has she contacted you? She must call her grandfather immediately to let him know where she is. Her family is ill with worry over her safety.'

'She can't do that, Ms Bardo. I received news that she has been in a car accident.'

Viola leaned back in her chair. This was one scenario that never crossed her mind. She imagined Nadia being held captive, or alone in some shelter or perhaps in digs with friends. Not this!

How on earth was she going to convey this news to Milsom? Too much — too soon.

'Car accident? Where? Is she gravely injured?'

'I'm afraid she is and is undergoing spinal surgery at Priory Hospital in the city. Hospital staff found my details in a notebook among her possessions and called me.'

'Thank you for reaching out. I will inform her family right away. You are a good friend to Nadia, Tamarind.'

'Thank you, Ms Bardo, I'm glad I called you. Please let me know how things go. I don't want to trouble Nadia's family.'

'I will. You take care now. Hope to see you back at the Academy soon.'

Viola returned to her office to find a patient Maida still waiting for her.

'Viola, you look terrible. White as a sheet!'

'I have a few urgent calls to make. I've had some disturbing news that I cannot discuss. And I might have to speak to the mayor.'

'Corey? Whatever for? Don't rely on him for anything, trust me.'

Maida's vehemence, the voice of old residents of Blackwater Ridge, came as no surprise. Viola called her PA to attend to Maida and walked over to see Milsom in person at Cesario Lane Bakery. The store was still shut, but Milsom worked at the back.

'Ms Bardo! This is a surprise. I am sorry we are shut, I know you love your twice a week batch of fresh bread rolls. I could prepare them for you to pick up after work.'

Viola's heart pounded. Here was a lovely, considerate man about to receive terrible news from her while he struggled to come to terms with his granddaughter's disappearance. She wished she did not have to do this.

'Sorry for bursting in, Milsom. I had to see you in person. There's been some news about Nadia.'

Milsom clutched his chest.

'Have they have found her?'

Viola knew from his reaction that he was expecting the worst, but could not bring himself to ask.

'She's been in a car accident and is having surgery at Priory Hospital. I received this news a few minutes ago and rushed over to see you.'

'Accident?' His lifeless blue eyes looked past Viola.

Viola touched his arm.

'You should call the hospital and go up to Sydney. You must let the family know. I can come home with you to tell them the news.'

He shook his head.

'No, I'll do it. You have done enough with your load of demands in your busy day. Thank you for coming over. I appreciate all you have done.'

Milsom shuffled out the building, slowed down by this news.

Nadia had to pull through. She was the center of Milsom's universe. Milsom reminded her of her father in his devotion to family.

In Andy's family, things were settling down with Vivian's return. After hours of tears and arguments, Vivian's mother accepted that her daughter would remain a single parent. Vivian's father offered to help her with her confinement costs. He left his family to reclaim his wild days. Andy stepped in to tell him they did not need his help. The family had Vivian's back.

Viola wondered how this change would impact on a portion of the uptight attitude in this small community in Blackwater Ridge. Most were keen on change. A new set of values was ready to be born, to catch up with the rest of the nation. There was no shame in the truth's telling. Corey was truth's waning shadow. His leadership was about to topple. He would be a fool not to see it coming.

Phoebe Constantine packed her bags, quit TAFE, and headed back to her family in Tasmania. Until now, nobody knew that Nadia and Tamarind were friends. Youth knew how to adhere to the secrecy that their town's tight-lipped leadership demanded.

* * *

A FULL MEETING of the Academy's board convened, and they invited Andy to attend. Maida was ill with the flu and absent that evening.

Lawrence Hargreaves was not one to mince his words.

He thanked Andy for accepting the invitation, and for being a proactive member of the Academy's community in safely bringing the missing young women home.

'Look Andy, it's pointless skirting around issues. You may or may not know that Ms Bardo cannot take up our offer for permanent principalship here at the Academy. We are still trying to coerce her into joining the board.' He looked over at Viola and nodded. 'Ms Bardo has seconded our decision to offer you the principal position at Blackwater Ridge Performing Arts Academy.'

Andy looked at Viola for confirmation. She gave him a broad smile and a nod.

Hargreaves continued, 'How do you feel about this offer. I know it's sudden and we are putting you on the spot, but we need to know where you sit with this offer, as time is of the essence.

Your commitment and passion tell us you are the right person for the post.'

Andy could not comprehend this offer. There were many senior staff members who qualified and might want the opportunity to try for the spot.

'Are you advertising the position?'

'Oh yes, we are. The law requires it, and we abide.'

'Why offer me the position, now, before advertising?'

'We assume when advertised you will respond, and we will choose you as our favored candidate. Your credentials are flawless.'

'Thank you for your vote of confidence. I would rather it was a fair and just selection.'

'So will you apply once advertised?'

Andy shot Viola a glance.

'I will if I knew Ms Bardo was going to take on a role with the board.'

A scarlet faced Viola turned in surprise to Andy.

'I'm afraid I can't commit to that with some personal matters that demand my attention.'

Hargreaves was quick to respond. 'We can wait, Ms Bardo.'

The meeting dispersed, and Andy hurried over to Viola.

'What was that all about? You opt out and throw me into the hell-fire!'

'Nothing of the sort! I cannot stay in any permanent capacity, and the board has tremendous respect for you.'

'I see.'

'They won't let you go that easily, Ms Bardo. They will make you an offer you cannot refuse.'

'The only offer I need is flexibility, like I had under Rob's leadership.'

'Let's test it!'

Andy believed Viola would have a foot in Blackwater Ridge. She returned each time she left, happy to be back.

'And so, the waiting begins again. All I want is for Nadia Jones to be well again and reunited with her family.'

Waiting was Viola's way of life from her parents' decision to end their relationship and Lorenza's uncanny departure. Matthew Soto took a step forward, and she retreated, waiting to be sure of her heart.

Nadia was in good care — that waiting was bearable.

Waiting for the next round of news from Tempest darkened the circles around Viola's eyes.

30

The return call from Tempest never happened.

Her doctor advised rest with nothing stressful for a few days. The sword of Damocles dangled over Viola, exhausting her.

Three days passed like three years.

News arrived that Nadia was recovering from her surgery, but chances were she would never walk again. Milsom hung onto the strong-willed belief of the Jones' clan that his granddaughter would return to her old self.

Viola heard Milsom's determination in his words. He would sell Cesario Lane Bakery and do whatever he could to ensure Nadia had every opportunity for a full recovery. A man for whom family was the sun, moon, and stars.

THE NERVOUS WAIT for Tempest's call ended with an email notification on the day and time. An evening call was mutually accepted. As usual, Sebastian arrived an hour early. At the stroke of the allotted hour, Tempest appeared. Her breathing was easier, and her lawyer, Richard of *Richard and Monroe and Associates* said she might hold up for longer this evening. Viola sipped a cup of coffee, relaxed that the wait was over, and glad to see Tempest looking brighter in the eye and cheek.

'What are you sipping, Viola, coffee? I miss it, I tell you.'

'Oops, sorry Tempest, let me put this mug out of sight to avoid tempting you!'

'Go ahead, I'm a big girl! Well, a withering away big girl!' She tried to laugh and coughed instead.

'How are you, Tempest?' Sebastian asked and got two thumbs up and a big smile.

Tempest turned her head to look at Sebastian.

'What I have to say today is for you, Sebastian, but it is inter-twined with Viola in this narrative.'

Viola was in awe of Tempest's grace and dignity in how she articulated her thoughts even as she battled with her health.

'Before Lorenza left for the safe house, she made me promise that I would visit Placido, check out how he was doing and report it to my brother, Bernado, who would pass the message on to her. Your father meant everything to her, Viola. Know that, but I sense you already do.'

Viola nodded, and Sebastian waited for his part of the emerging story to unfold. He felt as though he were standing on a cliff with a steep, foggy drop below. He was still — breathing like a newborn babe.

'It was a few months after Lorenza left when I could make that visit. I attended one of Placido's open nights in his early days at *Galleria Bardo*. I was a stranger, and he could not be told about my connection to Lorenza. For his own safety.'

She paused for a drink of water. Her doctor swabbed her forehead. Tempest raised her hand to signal she was ready to go on.

'Remember, all I was there to do was to assess if he was ok. Lorenza said what he did not know about her situation would spare him the torment of knowing why she had to leave. It was imperative to her that the people hunting her believed she was dead. My brother made sure of that.'

Viola's emotions dipped and dived, bringing her to the brink of tears each time Lorenza's name came up. She thought she was stronger now, but the terror Lorenza underwent to protect her, and her father, returned like a haunting.

'Placido noticed I was alone. He came up to me as I walked around and got chatting about my interest in art. He invited me to join his private dinner party at his gallery residence.'

Viola was agog that Tempest was a visitor in her home, dining with her father and his closest associates.

'When Placido knew of my Mozambican ancestry, he asked me to stay on for drinks after his guests left to chat about the old days there. I asked pertinent questions to deliver his responses as directed by Lorenza. He told me about his painful divorce and the shattering blow of his sister's disappearance.'

Tempest paused for a sip of water. Her doctor hovered in the background with a watchful eye. Viola was aware the conversation was being recorded.

'Now that I have clarified that, here is the part I hope you both don't judge unkindly.'

Sebastian was statue still.

Viola expected him to nod or acknowledge what Tempest had just said.

'I spent the night with Placido. We were two lonely souls. I left before he rose in the morning. He had no way of contacting me. I was mindful not to leave any leads.'

Tempest paused again.

'I struggled with halting the urge to call him, but had to respect Lorenza's wishes. She chose self-exile to protect him. I

could not sully that. Two months later, I confirmed I was pregnant. I was carrying Placido's child.'

Viola's heart thumped so hard her chest ached.

'I sent word to my brother about all that had happened. I
have his response with me and a letter he attached from Lorenza.
With your permission, may I ask Richard to read her letter out.'

Sebastian responded, 'Please go ahead if Viola agrees.'

Viola nodded with her palms clasped.

My Dear Tempest,

*I am terribly sorry for your current situation, but for my
part it comforts me in knowing that my beloved Placido is safe.
Thank you from the bottom of my heart. How I wish you could
be with him. I have one request, but it is your final decision.
Please have his child, and only when the time is right, tell him
and my darling Viola. If this poses a threat to you, please opt
out for your safety first. If it is meant to be, Viola will know she
is not alone.*

Viola's heart-wrenching sobs were audible. She stood up and
walked to the window and back. Sebastian was helpless,
confused, and not sure what to say or ask.

'Where is this child or person? Did you have, papa's child?
Please tell me.'

Tempest closed her eyes for a few seconds. Tears twinkled
like stars in the wrinkled crevices of her eyes.

'Viola, Sebastian is your brother, my son.'

Sebastian rushed out the room. He stood on the balcony; his
chest ready to burst from being walled up for a lifetime. How
could Tempest have forsaken him, her child, begot one night
after too many glasses of wine? His body was weightless. The

town lights on the horizon were a blur of tears. He sat on the cold tiled floor and sobbed for all that he believed to be true – now shattered. Who was he?

Viola walked out to him, and whispered, 'Come inside, please, we need to talk.'

She led him back to the lounge room like a docile, lost child.

He looked at the black screen. 'Where's Tempest?'

'She will call you for a private chat soon.'

Sebastian looked at Viola with bloodshot eyes, his head drumming repeatedly with what he just heard.

'Why, after all this time, when I spent decades crying for my mother to come and get me, she returns now? My adoptive parents were lovely, but I never felt whole, complete, you know.'

'Hush, Sebastian. All you are feeling is real. I know it is a huge ask, but please don't judge Tempest. Fate conspired, and she did the best she could.'

Sebastian rocked back and forth, a child again. One who had lost everything.

'We have each other, Sebastian. We are family. If ever I wanted a brother, it would be you. I would choose you.'

Sebastian walked over to Viola and hugged her.

'You are all the family I need,' he whispered between sobs. 'I should not be sad.'

'You are sad about what you have missed in knowing who you are. We can bridge that gap together. But please do not hate Tempest. She brought us together.'

'No, I don't hate her for what has happened. Please believe me.'

'Good! With Tempest's permission we must let my father, our papa, know that he has a son. This will be a massive shock to him. We have to think through how we are going to break this to him... perhaps face-face is the way.'

'I'm not thinking that far ahead. I am in shock. I am afraid of how I will react in Placido's presence.'

'It won't be right away. You must have time to process it all first. Take advice from Tempest on how to proceed. '

'I agree.'

Tempest arranged a private call with Sebastian. She granted permission to Viola and Sebastian to tell Placido in whatever way they chose.

3 1

And so it came to pass that two only adult children had one father.

Divorce and adoption, both painful childhoods for Viola and Sebastian, and the twist of fate, somehow orchestrated by Lorenza and Tempest, made them sister and brother. Vigilante agents received family justice, long overdue to them, but here.

SEBASTIAN UNDERSTOOD the cruel hand of fate in his birth, and why his mother had to play by the rules to buy him and his father safety. Lorenza's fight for justice attracted underworld attention, ending her right to freedom. When the freedom and safety of loved ones are threatened, love removes the seat of threat. Good families, united by unconditional love, sacrificed themselves for the greater family good.

The truth hung between Viola and Sebastian like a hot-air balloon fired to reach their father.

Two truths Placido had yet to face.

For now, they went about the daily business of life.

* * *

Nadia Jones returned to Blackwater Ridge in a wheelchair, determined to walk again. Milsom sold Cesario Lane Bakery and spent all his days with his granddaughter, taking her for physiotherapy, breakfasts, and dinners. He began the process for a youth center for Blackwater Ridge's idle youth. It would be a place where youngsters could hang out for clean fun. He commissioned a gaming arcade, a bowling alley and mini movie theater. He had a fight on his hands with some townsfolk when he wanted to include a dance club.

Tamarind Jenkins returned to the Academy and agreed to be an inspirational speaker on youth affairs. The board funded her training in that area. Rick Mantel offered to assist her and Milsom to manage the upcoming youth center.

The first soon to be single mother in Blackwater Ridge no longer hid herself away. Her mother became her ardent supporter.

And much to Viola's relief, Andy accepted the position of acting principal for now, he said. He needed to test his leadership skills before he committed to anything permanent.

Good old persistent Maida Halliwell convinced Viola, to accept a board role with the proviso that she was at liberty to come and go as she desired.

'In this world we must use the technology available to us to zoom you in from any part of the world. We need female representation on the board. Truth, be told, I am not going to be around forever!'

Maida's refreshing honesty and forward thinking, beyond her years, added a ring of truth to Rob declaring her the only jewel on the Academy's board.

* * *

VIOLA AND SEBASTIAN thought through how they would break
the news to Placido — he had a newfound, long lost, unknown to
him, son. Viola cringed when she thought about her father's
lapsing memory. Would he recall the night he spent with
Tempest? If he didn't, it would destroy Sebastian's hope to have
a family with the same blood flowing in his veins. Then there
was the question of her name. Was Tempest her proper name?
Did Placido know that name? In all her years, under her justice
boss lady, her father showed no interest in wanting to know who
Tempest was. Viola's vigilante work was off limits for any
discussion, and he respected that.

'I'm not comfortable sitting in on the first conversation you
have with your father... our father about my existence.'

Sebastian's mournful look tugged at her.

'Papa would want to talk to you, and Tempest might not
withstand the stress of talking directly to him. And I won't
suggest she does.'

'She's stronger than you give her credit for, even now. Look
at all she endured alone, for so long.'

'Yeah, but she is older now. We accept that.'

Viola's wise beyond her years advice spoke of her as one
who had lived for a century.

'I understand, but how do we tell Placido if we are only
going to Porto in September? That is four months away! What if
this leaks to the media before we get to him? He is a celebrity in
the art world.'

Viola glared at Sebastian, primed for a sibling attack.

'How is that ever going to happen unless one of us leaks it to
the press? Let me tell you, such negligence disrespects what

Lorenza sacrificed to protect papa. The situation last year with Mural Man is proof that he is still vulnerable to attack.'

Viola's angry outburst shocked Sebastian.

'Please don't think, for one second that I would do such a thing. I am disappointed that you appear to be suggesting that. Such unfounded anger does not become you, Viola!'

Viola heaved when she realized she had overreacted.

'I'm glad you know how protective I am of papa. I am sorry if I gave you that impression. I said it with no malice to you.'

'Good, let's make it clear, that we are not out to hurt each other. We know little bother's get their ears boxed by older sisters.'

'Or the other way around!'

Viola's suggestion riled Sebastian when she suggested asking Matthew to visit Placido when they told him the Bardo family news. She explained her father was a sensitive man and not in the best of health.

It dawned upon her that Sebastian, too, was a sensitive fellow.

'Like father, like son,' slipped out before she could hold her tongue.

'What's that?'

'Nothing.'

'You said it, so explain it. I am the son, so it can't be Matthew you're referring to.'

'Don't fly off the handle on this, but I just realized you have papa's sensitive side.'

'Flying off the handle must be a family trait too, then!' Sebastian grinned. 'You make this judgement because I confided in you about my sad childhood when we met in Athens.'

'Hey, we are family, no secrets, no sadness, no arguments. Let's celebrate. Gin?'

'Yes, please! Got to calm these nerves!'

* * *

VIOLA CALLED MATTHEW, with Sebastian's approval. He stepped out onto the balcony to give her space.

'Viola, lovely to hear from you. Congratulations on your decision to stick to what you want from life!'

It was not an appropriate time to tell him her arm was twisted to embrace the part-time board position. In the emotional turbulence of Tempest's revelation, she neglected to update Matthew on the board's last request.

'So, what are your plans for returning to Porto?'

She thanked the universe for this entry to her request.

'Ideally I would like to be there in person to share some family news with papa.'

Matthew's signature silence marked his awkwardness.

'I have a favor to ask, which I seem to do often. If this makes you uncomfortable or you cannot commit, please know you can refuse without ruining the friendship.'

'Friendship? Anything to help Placido is a pleasure. He is a grand man with a heart of gold.'

She thanked him, but felt her insignificance in his allegiance to her father.

'Matthew, this is a big ask. Are you able to go to Porto to be with papa when I break some sensitive family news to him?'

Another awkward silence.

'Do you want me to be privy to your family's *sensitive* news? That makes me uncomfortable, but I would go in a heartbeat to support your papa through whatever it is.'

Sebastian stepped back inside and heard Matthew's response. He rushed to the kitchen, grabbed the notepad and pen from the side of the microwave and waved a scribbled note in front of Viola.

Do not tell him the actual news, please.

She nodded.

'I understand, Matthew, but would it help if I kept you in the dark on that piece of news? I'll leave it to papa to tell you, should he choose to?'

Silence…

'Yes... er... perhaps… May I ask, is this related to the crime at *Galleria Bardo* last year?'

'Not at all, this is a family matter of an extremely sensitive nature and because papa is fond of you, I thought it best to ask for your help to support him through it.'

Matthew knew how to drag things out. She wanted this tied up, and the day for her call to her father settled.

'I will assist however you want me to, and it will be Placido's choice to tell me or not.'

Viola's inner sigh almost gave away her relief.

'Thank you, very much, Matthew. I will work around what time suits you. Let me know when you can go over to Porto. I will arrange the rest and notify you.'

'I can go over next weekend. I have a nanny in residence now for Jungen. He adores her. But, not as much as he adores you.'

'Are you a hundred percent sure that you are comfortable doing this? I could ask papa's cousin, Madelena, to look after Jungen if you take him along to Porto. He enjoyed being around her children during your Christmas visit.'

Sebastian shook his head and raised his hands in protest. He scribbled on the notepad again.

Do not drag anyone else into this!

'It's best I leave him with the nanny here. Your papa might need to be calm and undisturbed. Jungen is quite demanding of his attention.'

'Thank you for your understanding. That's settled. If you are there by Saturday, I will call papa on Sunday after he has had some time to settle into your visit.'

'Thank you. I will arrange everything today and call Placido to let him know of my impromptu visit.'

Viola trusted Matthew would soften the blow her father was about to receive.

'Phew, I can't believe that's settled!'

'It's far from settled for me.'

'I know, but we are lucky to have a friend like Matthew to help us out.'

'He's doing it to please you, you know that.'

Viola knew no comment was best when Sebastian was morose.

She sent a message to Tempest on her plan and received her blessing to go ahead.

Her message read:

This will set Placido and Sebastian free. I owe them the truth.
Be gentle with them both.

After Sebastian left, a restless Viola pondered why fate had dealt this hand. Her father would have been happy in a union with Tempest.

Fate was its own master, and mere mortals swayed to its command.

A thought infiltrated on how Helena would react to this well-kept secret. She tossed it aside, knowing that the tense situation and circumstances had no room for criticism.

3 2

Viola made the call to her father.

Matthew's unplanned visit was an excellent distraction for him.

She told him she had some news to share and asked if he was comfortable having Matthew around when she told him.

'Is this about Lorenza, meu filho?'

'Not quite. Some things have come to my attention, but are you comfortable with Matthew being around when we talk?'

'What is *not quite*? Either, it is, or it isn't. Why wait? Tell me now, I don't think I can bear waiting. You will only do this if it is serious stuff. I know my Artista.'

'It's something I have to gather more information on before I tell you.'

Viola had never deliberately lied to her father before. It was necessary to stall his curiosity to preserve his equanimity and wellbeing.

'I see. Yes, I am happy to have Matthew around. He is like a son and a friend, you know. He is a good man.'

Viola's heart skipped a beat, but she had to stay strong. She considered excluding Sebastian from her first conversation with Placido on Tempest's revelation, but transparency was vital after decades of secrecy. Nothing she had to say was unknown to him. He needed to trust how the news was being shared. Placido's reaction was her primary concern.

* * *

TWO DAYS PASSED FASTER than she expected. Matthew sent her a message when he was in the taxi on his way to *Galleria Bardo*. He had a day to settle in with her father before she called him. She could trust Matthew to steer Placido away from asking what he knew about this 'news' his Artista wanted to share.

THAT SUNDAY MORNING, Viola's lounge room was again a place where secrets came to be received and told.

Sebastian sat on the couch opposite her when she made the call.

'Artista, prompt as ever. I have had my breakfast and Matthew is here. I wish you were here too. Out with it, let me hear the news you have.'

'I'm coming over in September. Maybe Matthew can make another trip to Porto then.'

'It's a deal. Matthew is nodding in agreement, meu filho.'

Viola knew the small talk had to end for serious matters to take its place.

'Papa, I need to jog your memory here. Do you recall meeting a Portuguese Mozambican woman on one of your early eighties opening nights at the gallery?'

'You are definitely not talking about your mother because she has French blood in her veins.' He laughed, unsure why Viola was asking him to remember someone from three decades ago.

196

'No, not mother. A stranger, who came over for your exhibition when you launched Lorenza's portrait.'

'Why do you ask, Artista? It was a long time ago.'

'Because she has contacted me.'

'Rosana contacted you? Why? I met her once and never heard from her again.'

The name *Rosana* slipped out as though she were always on his mind — certainly not a ghost from his past.

Viola could not hold back any longer.

'She wanted you to know that the night you spent together brought your son into being.'

Sebastian rested his head in his left hand.

Dead silence, followed by deep breathing and the sound of Matthew's voice asking if Placido wanted a drink of water.

'Papa, are you, ok?'

'I am meu filho, I am, but I'm sorry I never mentioned Rosana to you. She left without saying goodbye, and I had no way of contacting her. Like Lorenza, you know. She could have told me about the child. I would have loved him and raised him. Why did she keep it a secret? I felt drawn to her when I met her. She had class and compassion. Please believe me.'

Viola heard the anguish in her father's voice and Sebastian's soft sob.

'I do, papa. Rosana is not well and wanted you to know that you are the father of the son she had. She is happy for you to get to know him if that is your wish. She has struggled with keeping this from you.'

A long pause followed.

'Meu filho, how do you feel about me meeting him, my son, your brother, that I did not know existed?'

'This is your choice, papa. Do you want to meet your son?'

It was important to Viola that Sebastian heard this directly from Placido.

Heart-wrenching sobs followed. Her father cried for what he

never knew and for a daughter who wanted nothing but his happiness.

'I do, meu filho. I want to see him, know him, tell him I am sorry I did not know of his arrival in this world. I hope he believes me, or that he wants to meet me, or whether I will be his father, now.'

Sebastian sobbed unashamedly, a lost boy, finding his father for the first time when he heard Placido's tearful question.

'What is my boy's name, meu filho?'

'Papa, you remember I told you about agent Sebastian who worked with me in Athens, he is right here with me. Sebastian is my brother's name.'

Viola was in control up to this point. She broke down now and clung to Sebastian.

It would have to be another time when she told her father that Rosana was Tempest, and why she kept this secret close to her heart.

'Would you like to speak to him, papa?'

'I want to, but I'm a sniveling mess. What will he think of me?'

'Like father like son, papa...'

Viola heard Matthew say, 'Speak to your son. He won't mind your tears. That's family love.'

Matthew's support and encouragement comforted Viola. She was glad her father had a good man with him to support him through this news.

Sebastian reached for the phone and put it to his ear. He wanted this moment to be his alone.

'Mr Bardo. It is Sebastian, sir.'

'Sebastian, what a beautiful name! Will you call me papa? I cannot wait to meet you, my son.'

'Likewise papa. And thank you for accepting me with no doubts or suspicions, and thank you for my beautiful sister.'

'You are my son, I do not doubt that. Artista, is indeed beautiful inside and out.'

Both spoke for a short while through undulating emotions, until Matthew took the phone from Placido to speak to Viola.

'You have done well, Viola. You take care of Sebastian and I will ensure your papa is ok here. We are going to put our heads together to get you and Sebastian here soon.'

'How do I even begin to thank you?'

'You already have, by trusting me.'

He clicked off, and Sebastian gave her the biggest boyish grin she had ever seen.

She knew, had the circumstances been different, Sebastian would have teased her about Matthew's devotion to her.

'So much down. The truth sure does set you free.'

Sebastian called Tempest, wanting to share the news of connecting with his father. There was no delay in her picking up his call. Her phone was close at hand ever since she released the truth that had kept her restless for decades.

Tempest sighed in relief when Sebastian thanked her.

'How blessed am I, to have found both my parents after all these years of imagining who they were? Thank you.'

Viola knew her father's old-world values prevented him from telling her he had met a woman he knew intimately for one night.

Nothing mattered now.

The Bardo's were united as family.

The load had lifted off Tempest's shoulders. She had to work through how she would reveal Lorenza's situation to Placido.

* * *

Autumn passed in Blackwater Ridge, and the first icy blast of winter crept in during the first two days of June. Viola and Sebastian confirmed they would go to Porto in July. Sebastian applied for an extension of his sabbatical and another six months' leave of absence without pay. This would allow him to have quality time with Placido.

Blackwater Ridge rolled into a calm period.

Many meetings went on behind closed doors with Ellis, Corey, Andy, Milsom and the police commissioner.

Mayor Corey stepped back from his position, and a young city man arrived to take over the reins. Change had arrived in this small, tight-lipped community. Some secrets were best left alone in the name of progress.

* * *

By the end of June, Tempest was back in her island home.

She wheeled herself out onto the balcony to cast her eyes across the landscape. The fog had lifted, and the sun peeped through soft shifting balls of cloud to warm her. Woza and Khaya curled pressed up against her wheelchair. Khaya's head found its way onto Tempest's foot.

This view was her comfort during her decades of solitude. She sat back with the sun on her head and was soon sound asleep. Caramba, perched on the balcony bannister, flew over and settled down on the backrest of her wheelchair.

A purple blanket lay draped across her legs.

Sebastian gently touched his mother's head and stepped back inside the cottage.

He returned an hour later to take her back in, when the air had cooled down, she was still sound asleep, just as he had left her.

He felt her forehead.

She was cold.

And so Tempest departed before her son could meet his father.

EPILOGUE

The scattering of Tempest's ashes in the ocean was a still day down at her favorite haunt. Caramba swooped overhead without a sound, but with a watchful eye on how his beloved was laid to rest, Woza and Khaya curled on the sand, morose. Strewn flowers decorated the footpath down to the beach Tempest had walked along every morning for over three decades, Viola wrote in the sand:

you blew into my life
a tempest from afar
gone but forever near
your laughter heard
dancing in the wind
the ocean rolling
with your caramel tones
eternal — forever near

Sebastian urged her to have the words inscribed on a wall plague which he nailed on the balcony wall facing a perfect view of the ocean from Tempest's favorite chair.

Placido never spoke of Rosana again, and Helena cut all contact with him. Sebastian and Placido spent many hours talking art and catching up on their missed years.

* * *

FIVE YEARS PASSED like five brief summers after a lengthy winter.

Tempest had decades to put her house in order. She worked with *Richard Monroe and Associates* for many years, ensuring that Sebastian was in want of nothing. Time would ensure her son and his father were safe from harm. She denied herself the joy of motherhood and the love of a man who ignited her heart like no other. Sometimes, just one night is magical enough to sustain the darkness that follows. Marriages ended in disaster. Hers was a love she carried to her grave. Honoring her promise was more important than fulfilling her personal desires.

She untangled the truth when time ran out on her.

Tempest's island home was in Sebastian's name. She signed the deed to the house and property in the month of his birth. His birth certificate bore Placido Bardo's name as his biological father, not father unnamed like that of an accidental birth.

In her last will and testament, she bequeathed *TT Justice Agency* to Viola and Sebastian. She hoped for them to carry forth the torch to rectify the ills of the world. Tempest appointed Viola to head the agency. A list of Tempest's closest contacts revealed their promise to continue to support the cause.

Viola spent six months of the year in Porto and six months in Sebastian's island home. Matthew and Jungen visited both homes whenever they could. Matthew's relationship with Viola continued in their warm closeness — nothing more expected of each other. Her fear of commitment was deep-seated. This way, they had each other for life. Viola and Sebastian dedicated their lives to keeping Placido's life normal and comfortable. Their beautiful father lived out his days at *Galleria Bardo*, unable to travel to his children's island home, but happy that they were together.

They were both the children of their father's home.

While one old secret was free to roam, and Tempest's private journals were discovered in the attic, all her deepest desires now had wings.

She was free.

Blackwater Ridge's mining secret went to the grave with Mayor Corey. Viola gave up her position on the board at the Academy to devote her life to poetry, justice, and family.

And of Lorenza, nothing more came to light.

I have unclasp'd to thee the book even of my secret soul…
  Twelfth Night — William Shakespeare

AFTERWORD

My passion for teaching and writing are closely aligned hence I thought I would share my perceptions on the role of teachers and why I had this vision of Viola Bardo as teacher and justice seeker.

Teaching is never singular in the manifold duties of the role as educator, nurturer, social justice initiator, carer, and person that a child/student/peer can trust. In my growing up years I have been blessed to have had teachers who opened my ears and eyes beyond the confines of a narrow-minded apartheid system. Equally, my parents ensured that apartheid did not define the course of my life. It is as a consequence of my visionary mentors, the wonderful schools I attended, and the friendships forged that I uphold :

In our angst and joy we are ONE under the sky of humanity.

Within perceived or self-labeled imperfection lies a wealth of perfection. Teachers celebrate and grow this wealth in their students.

Fundamental to the role of a teacher is respect for all. This in turn generates self-respect and cradles students to exude the same.

All Lives Matter is drawn into my stories from this foundation of my teaching and childhood experience growing up in apartheid South Africa. Nobody should suffer the fate of a black child born on the wrong side of apartheid. Nowhere in the world.

Relationships are core to leadership and every teacher, every upholder of peace and justice regardless of the occupation they inhabit is a significant cog to a safe and secure society.

The fictional character, Viola Bardo, emulates the multifaceted duties of a teacher with music in her blood and the capacity to selflessly serve others.

The characteristics Viola Bardo portrays make her a role-model for all who go through the difficulties she did as a child — living through the acrimonious divorce of her parents, having an absent, yet controlling mother, enduring grief and family revelations that challenge her in her yearning for family.

DO YOU ENJOY TRILOGIES?

If you enjoy trilogies, the *Souls of Her Daughters Collection* may be read as a trilogy or as standalone novels.

Dr Grace Sharvin, and her social worker sister escape from South Africa to Australia. The past cannot be undone on their quest for a new life. Meet the mothers, sisters and friends from a global cast of fictional characters as they share their heartfelt angst and joy with the reader.

Can a mother's love save her daughters from an unforgettable past?

A secret global mission to end domestic violence.

Two sisters from different cultural backgrounds, each on a humanitarian mission, will a love interest test their bond?

If you've enjoyed reading, *Blackwater Mornings - (The Bardo Trilogy 3)* please leave an honest review to help other readers decide if they might like to read my books. This will help me to write more.

With Gratitude,

Mala Naidoo
www.malanaidoo.com

9 780648 809043